The Chronicles of Avantia

With special thanks to Stephen Chambers

For Calvin

www.chroniclesofavantia.com

ORCHARD BOOKS
338 Euston Road, London NW1 3BH
Orchard Books Australia
Level 17/207 Kent St, Sydney, NSW 2000

A Paperback Original
First published in Great Britain in 2010

Chronicles of Avantia is a registered trademark of Beast Quest Limited
Series created by Working Partners Limited, London

Text © Beast Quest Limited 2010
Cover and inside illustrations by Artful Doodlers, with special thanks
to Bob. © Orchard Books 2010

A CIP catalogue record for this book is available from
the British Library.

ISBN 978 1 40830 748 9

9 10 8

Printed and bound by CPI Group (UK) Ltd, Coydon, CR0 4YY

The paper and board used in this paperback are natural recyclable
products made from wood grown in sustainable forests.
The manufacturing processes conform to the environmental
regulations of the country of origin.

Orchard Books is a division of Hachette Children's Books,
an Hachette UK company.

www.hachette.co.uk

Chasing Evil

By Adam Blade

ORCHARD

www.chroniclesofavantia.com

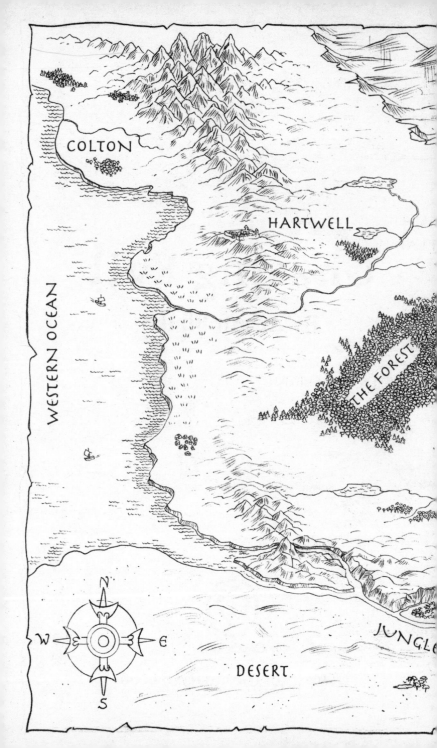

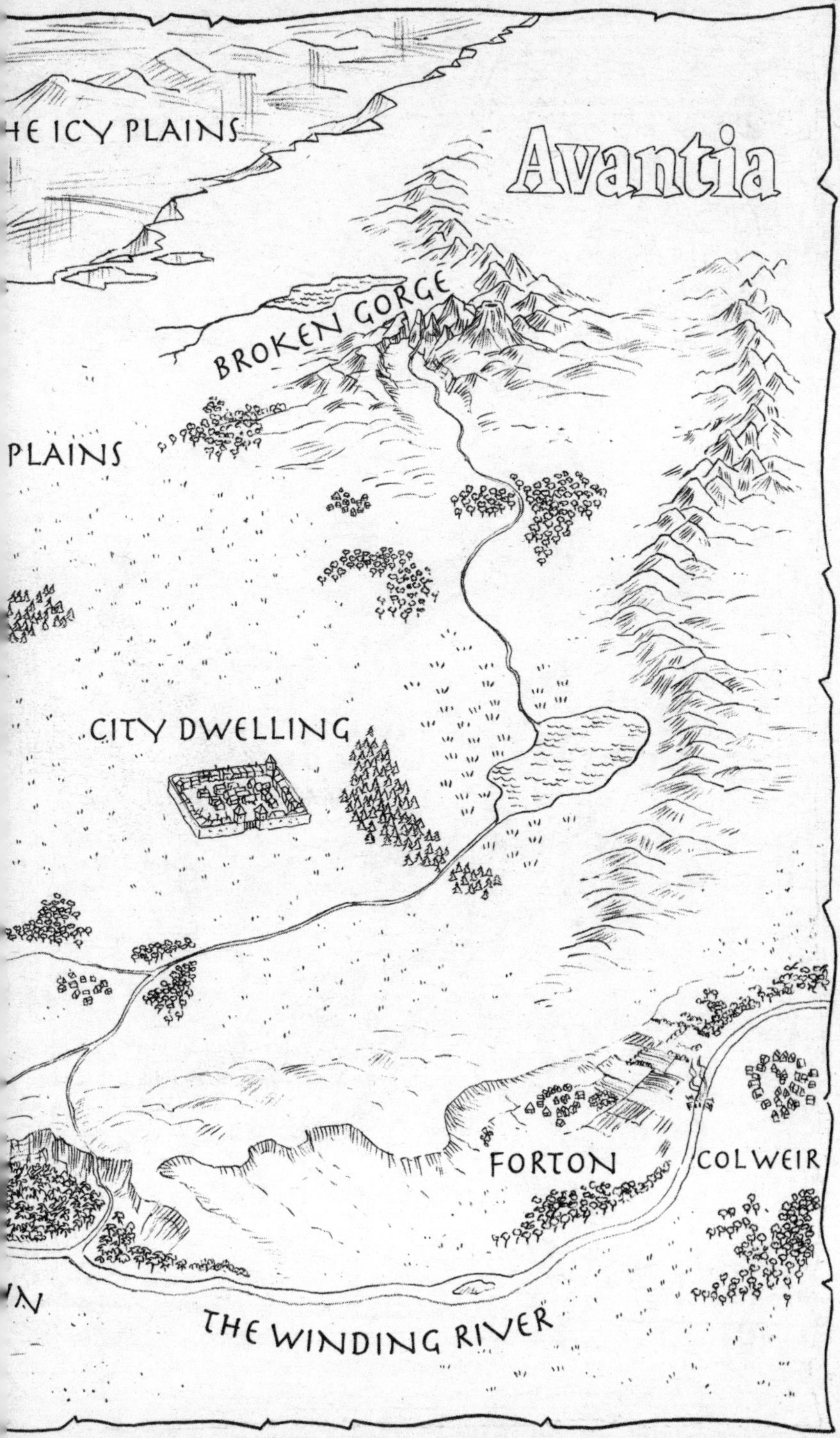
HE ICY PLAINS
Avantia
BROKEN GORGE
PLAINS
CITY DWELLING
FORTON
COLWEIR
N
THE WINDING RIVER

Destiny unfolds

Prologue

When I heard her laughter, I felt certain that she was my Chosen Rider. I was prowling in the high grass as the sun came up. I knew the world had colours, but I didn't know what that meant – I couldn't see them.

My eyes see things differently to humans. To me, daylight is white, and shadows and shapes are like grey shades, which turn to black. The morning air tasted like water-rock mist. I could smell the children, and, as I crept closer to peer through the waving grass, I saw a girl and her twin brother splashing in a river outside a village. I could hear every rustle in the grass, every drop of water fall. I could even smell the way their tunics moved and shifted, releasing their skin's scent.

'Gwen,' the boy called. 'You can't catch me!'

So that was her name. Gwen. As she laughed again – a beautiful, rippling noise, like a current in the air – I knew that I was right: she was my Chosen Rider. I'd found her! I knew it in the same way that I knew winter always follows autumn. This was deeper than a feeling;

it was fate. It was as Firepos had predicted.

'Geffen!' Gwen cried out to her brother. 'I'll get you!' Then she paused, and looked in my direction. She squinted in the sunlight. Somehow, she knew I was there.

'Gwen?' Geffen said. 'What's wrong?'

I walked out of the grass to the edge of the river. Geffen grabbed his sister. I snorted and tensed, unfolding my leathery wings from my back, casting huge shadows over the children.

'A Beast!' Geffen said. 'A wolf monster…' He scrambled away from me, shoving his sister in front of him, using her as a shield. Wide, frightened eyes watched me from behind her shoulder. That's when I knew for the first time: Geffen was a coward.

'It's all right,' Gwen said. She stepped closer to me.

'Don't!' Geffen said, drawing her back, but Gwen shook him off.

'Stay there,' she said. 'I'll be fine.'

Reluctantly, he nodded. Gwen came nearer, raising her hand towards me. I could smell her brother's acid fear, and under that, Gwen's calmness.

'Gulkien,' she said. 'That's your name.'

She knew me, in the same way I had known her when I heard her voice – the same way the sun knew to rise in the morning. This was the way the world worked; this was destiny.

I lowered myself to let her climb through my fur, and onto my back. She settled comfortably, as if she had been doing so for years. As I stood tall and opened my wings, my shadow dropped over Geffen. He smelt like terror, and I heard his heartbeat racing, faster and faster. Silly child.

'Gwen—' he began.

'It's all right,' she said again. 'Stay here, Geffen. I'm safe. And don't tell anyone!' She gave him a reassuring smile, as if to tell him what I already understood. She is not afraid. She always felt this was part of her fate. She rested a hand in my fur, and her eyes widened as she took in my huge wings. I flexed them for her, so that she could see how powerful her Beast was.

'I never dreamt you would be so beautiful,' she murmured.

I braced my hind legs and lunged into the air, my

wings beating hard, disturbing the river in a rush of air. She grasped my fur tightly. I flew high to show her my speed, and as we raced above a flock of geese, I dropped and opened my jaws—

'No!' Gwen shouted.

I pulled back and the geese scattered, honking. They smelt like dirty feathers and meat.

'You were going to kill those birds for sport,' she said. 'I won't let you do that, do you understand?'

I growled. Geese were senseless animals: prey. Couldn't she smell them? But if that was what she asked, I would obey. Even here, in the wet clouds, she wasn't frightened. Her heartbeat sounded so steady; it was as if she had been expecting me.

The clouds broke, and her pulse quickened.

'Oh, it's wonderful,' Gwen murmured. 'Look at the ground, so far below us – I've never seen it like this. I can see the whole curl of the river, and the sunlight is so orange and red along the edge of those hills.'

I looked: the river was a black line, and the hills were hazy and grey, cut with splits of white sunlight. I could smell the earth, and hear the grass rippling, the water rushing, but I couldn't see it as she did. I was glad to have her with me.

We followed the Deep River to soft mountain springs. I felt her shift on my back as she gazed around us.

We acted as one, with me as her guide and protector. My Chosen Rider, my Gwen.

Geffen's betrayal is discovered

Chapter One

Timbers creaked and crashed into the inferno, showering orange sparks. A fire in the building!

Tanner fell back, choking. How could he have let it happen? The sound of laughter made him look up.

A shadow appeared in the midst of the fire. A dark shape, moving. A survivor.

The figure stepped out of the flames. Black armour, cracked and smoking. The warrior wore a dark cloak, and carried a blood-caked sword. Innocent blood. His face was pale, with a heavy brow, and thin lips twisted into a sneer. One dark eye watched Tanner, the other was hidden behind a leathery piece of the Mask of Death. Derthsin. The warrior who had killed his father.

Tanner couldn't move as his enemy strode towards him. Every limb felt powerless. Derthsin lifted the sword above his head, and the bronze blade gleamed dimly.

'All of the mask will be mine!' he bellowed.

Tanner knew he was going to die.

The sword descended with a deadly hiss, slicing the air.

Tanner jolted awake. Stars were shining above him. His Beast, Firepos, stirred against his back. Her feathers shimmered gold beneath the moon and she dipped her huge beak to rest her head against Tanner's shoulder. The forest below smelt like pine and wet dirt, and a moonlit mist hung in the air. In the trees, the songbirds were roosting and no wind rustled the branches. Even the night noises of owls and crickets were absent.

Derthsin wasn't here. It had been a bad dream; that was all.

The sweat cooled on Tanner's skin, and he shivered. His grandmother used to say that dreams revealed deep and dark secrets. Grandmother Esme was dead now; killed by Derthsin's general, Gor. Tanner had held her body in his arms as blood bubbled from her wounds.

Tanner thought back to his village of Forton,

the destroyed home that he had left behind. *So much death, all in the name of Derthsin.* When Tanner was a boy, Derthsin had killed his father and kidnapped his mother. He had no idea where she was now but still thought of her – usually last thing before he fell asleep. Was she still out there, somewhere?

In revenge, Firepos had snatched up Derthsin and hurled him into the crater of the Stonewin volcano. Esme had told him this story over and over again. 'He fell to his death,' she had said. 'A death he deserved.' But she'd been wrong – Tanner knew that now. Derthsin had survived, clinging onto one of Firepos's feathers, tearing it from her to slow his fall. Now Derthsin had come back to Avantia in fiery visions, instructing General Gor to inflict more and more devastation on the land. He aimed to claim the Mask of Death once again. The mask would allow him to control all the Beasts of Avantia and beyond that – perhaps the kingdom? Tanner had no idea, but he knew it would be disastrous. He'd seen Derthsin's lust for power, tasted his evil. He wouldn't let that creature's dark influence stain his kingdom. *Not if I can stop it*, Tanner swore to himself. *I'd rather die.*

A few paces away, Gwen lay with her head nestled in Gulkien's fur. The wolf's massive flanks rose and fell gently as his leathery wings lay folded against his body. Until two days ago, Tanner had believed he was the only Chosen Rider in Avantia, but now he had a friend with her own Beast. As Esme died in his arms, his grandmother had sent him to find Jonas the Mapmaker in a neighbouring town. Tanner hadn't found Jonas, but he did find his adopted twins, Gwen and Geffen. He learnt that Jonas had been missing for many years.

Tanner and Gwen had already retrieved one piece of the mask, paying dearly for it. And Gwen had the secrets of the map that showed where the other pieces were, scattered across Avantia. Hidden in a locket that she wore at her throat was a piece of gauze. When she laid it over a map Jonas had left her, the locations of the mask pieces were revealed. If the two friends could keep going – if they could find the other three pieces of the mask – Derthsin would never have the power he lusted after.

Tanner watched Gwen sleep as he rested beside Firepos, the warmth from her feathers protecting him from the cold. He couldn't imagine how it would feel to be torn from Firepos, for his Flame Bird to answer to Derthsin. Beasts like Firepos and Gulkien were strong – not just with muscle, but with a powerful connection to this land and its people. Tanner had seen how Firepos could sense danger. Imagine if she became a creature of evil...

Avantia was already a kingdom of strangers – one village hardly ever saw its neighbours. Most people in the kingdom drew back from the Beasts, on the rare occasions they were spotted. What if the Beasts used this fear to drive people even further apart? Tanner shuddered.

Derthsin had armies, and he had Varlot – a true Beast of evil. Tanner would never forget his first sight of the Beast: half horse, half man, he was coated in armour, with terrifying bronze hooves that morphed into human hands, and long, strong fingers armed with vicious claws.

Tanner smelt a whiff of smoke and looked back into the cave. He saw the shape of a body beneath a blanket beside the campfire – Gwen's brother, Geffen. Geffen had been snatched by General Gor, but Gwen and Tanner had managed to rescue him from the suffocating embrace of the man's evil – even though, at the time, Geffen had thought he didn't want to be rescued.

We did the right thing, Tanner told himself. Gor had been swept away on an avalanche of water and rocks, created by Firepos. If they hadn't snatched Geffen, he'd be dead.

Embers smouldered and cast deep shadows

across the other boy's profile. The smoke thickened in low clouds and filled the air with the pungent smell of burning. Too much burning…

Tanner sprang up and ran into the cave. Geffen's blanket was on fire! Tanner could see that a stray ember had fallen onto it.

'Geffen!' he shouted.

But the boy didn't move.

'What is it?' asked Gwen, sitting up sleepily.

Tanner flung the blanket aside and revealed a pile of firewood arranged in the rough shape of a body. Tanner swivelled around, his eyes scanning the cave. Where was the piece of the mask that had lain beside the fire? Geffen had been looking at it last night, his eyes narrowed in concentration as he inspected the thick, leathery skin of the mask, hewn from an ancient Beast's face.

Tanner still shuddered whenever he saw the pieces of the mask – wizened skin as dark as coal, the shrunken crease of an eyelid and puckered lips peeled back in a wolfish grin. The Beast, Anoret, had once looked out from this face. Growing up, Tanner had heard stories about the first Beast of Avantia, born of fire. Legend had it that all other Beasts were descended from Anoret.

'Geffen?' said Gwen. Now fully alert, she leapt to her feet and drew her rapier. The braids in her white-blonde hair hung loosely.

'He's gone!' said Tanner, kicking the wood angrily across the cave. 'And he's taken the piece of the mask with him!'

Gwen rushed back to the cave entrance. She called out her brother's name over the trees beyond.

'Geffen! Geffen! Where are you? Come back!'

Gulkien, lifting his head, howled at her side. The wolf's lips curled back as he sent a call out across the air, his leathery wings stretching wide as he clambered to his feet. The wolf waited, his ears pricked. Nothing. He settled back down on the ground and looked at Gwen, licking his lips. His eyes spoke his understanding. Gulkien realised that Geffen had betrayed them. How long would Gwen take to accept it?

'We have to find him!' said Gwen. 'He might be in danger.'

Tanner shook his head. 'Don't you see? He's abandoned us and stolen the piece of the mask.'

Gwen frowned at him. 'No,' she muttered. 'He wouldn't do that.'

'You must have seen how he was looking at the mask last night,' said Tanner. 'He waited until we were all asleep, then scurried off like a rat. I *knew* we couldn't trust him.'

'Then why did you help rescue him? Don't talk nonsense. He's my brother – he wouldn't do this to me. To us.' Gwen's face was pale as she looked out over the landscape, her eyes scouring the horizon.

She can't bear to look at me, Tanner thought. *But in her heart, she knows I'm right.*

Beside her, Gulkien growled, lifting his black lips to reveal fangs as long as Tanner's hand. Warning him not to make Gwen even more upset.

Tanner looked out hopelessly over the forest and fields. Pink dawn was pushing back the black curtain of night, and pale clouds streaked the sky. Geffen could be anywhere.

'Well, whatever has happened,' said Tanner, 'we need to find him. And quickly.'

'Why?' Gwen spat. 'Because you're concerned for his welfare, or because you want your precious piece of mask back?'

'It's not my precious mask,' Tanner argued, 'I'm doing all this for the sake of Avantia. Or have you forgotten?'

Gwen shook her head in disgust. 'And why does Avantia need you, in particular? Geffen and I were happy before you arrived in our town. Now he's disappeared.'

'Happy? Your town was being attacked!' He couldn't believe that Gwen was being so stubborn.

Why wouldn't she accept that her brother had betrayed them? *I didn't ask for any of this either*, Tanner thought. He'd seen death, been torn from his home and forced into a fight against evil. He'd done exactly what had been asked of him – and more.

Gwen sheathed her rapier and went back into the cave. She snatched up Geffen's blanket and held it under Gulkien's snout. 'You'll help me, won't you?' she said. The wolf sniffed, his pale eyes widening as he took in the scent. Gwen put a hand on the fur of his neck and he lowered himself so she could climb onto his back, nestling into his thick fur.

'You take to the air and follow us,' she said coldly to Tanner, still not looking at him. 'We'll find his trail on the ground.'

Tanner nodded and hoisted himself into the space between Firepos's wings. The Flame Bird ruffled her feathers. With a nudge from Tanner's feet, she spread her mighty wings and sprang from the ledge, falling for a heartbeat before climbing into the dawn sky on thrusting wings.

Gulkien, with the thin membranes of his wings pressed tight against his body, leapt into the gorse below, scattering loose rocks. With perfect balance, he made his way down the steep slope, Gwen clinging tightly to his fur. At the bottom of the gorge, he paused at the tree line, nose close to the ground. Taut muscles shifted along the wolf's broad back. As Gulkien smelt the trees, he snorted. His eyes glittered like molten gold. He plunged into the trees with a spray of leaves and pine needles.

Tanner steered Firepos in pursuit, the wind blasting his face. The forest below was a dense, dark green. They soared higher, cutting through strands of pure, wet cloud. Beyond the forest lay fields of yellowing wheat, crisscrossed with dirt roads and animal paths. Avantia glowed in the morning sunlight, grass rippling like waves. But there was no sign of the boy.

Below them, Gulkien streaked across a forest clearing, then into the trees again. Even if Tanner couldn't see Geffen from up here, the scent down below must have been strong. Tanner's anger burned. *We've been through so much to find the mask. And now Gwen's brother has run off with the prize. Why?*

Beneath them, the trees ended. Gulkien paused, panting for breath. From Firepos's back, Tanner squinted into the sun. There was a shape on the far horizon – a tiny figure, running. Tanner felt in his tunic and pulled out his Looking Crystal. The oblong of opaque stone, inherited from his father, allowed him to see far into the distance. Lifting it to his eye, the swirling white faded away and a boy snapped into view. *Geffen!* Gwen's brother clutched the leathery fragment of Derthsin's mask in one hand. As Tanner watched, he disappeared over the crest of a hill.

Tanner swooped down, calling out to Gwen over the wind, 'I see him ahead. Follow me!'

Gwen urged Gulkien on and the Beast set off once more, racing with strides twenty paces long. They were approaching the low hill. Tanner squeezed Firepos's flanks and the Flame Bird beat her wings faster. He could sense the Beast's excitement. *We've almost got you!*

They broke over the crest of the hill. The sight made Tanner lurch back: hundreds of soldiers, formed into neat ranks, their arrows trained into the sky. They were led by the familiar silhouette of General Gor.

Tanner saw straight away that these troops were different from before. Some of the men had armour that was more highly polished, the tips of their spears glinting with the smooth metallic shine of weapons that had not yet seen warfare. Even from this distance, Tanner could see how fresh some of the men's faces were. *They're new recruits*, Tanner realised. As quickly as he'd defeated Gor's men in the mountains, the general had found replacements to bolster the missing soldiers from his army.

So Gor's still alive. Tanner had been certain that the general had died in the torrent during their last fight. And how had General Gor known where to meet Geffen? *Had he...* Tanner thought back to how Gor had failed to push Geffen out of Firepos's grasp. The Flame Bird had easily swept the boy up, to return him to his sister. *Too easily?* Had this been part of Gor's last, desperate plan – to let Geffen come back to his friends? Had the two of them planned this meeting place?

There was no time left to think. General Gor, mounted on his black stallion and wearing his dragon-snouted helmet, lifted his arm and pointed at Tanner.

He shouted, 'Loose!'

Battle in the skies

Chapter Two

Tanner sends a warning message, but I have seen the danger already. Tipping my wings, I arc away as a hundred arrows slice the sky. I climb and the shafts fall short, or bounce off my feathers harmlessly. This day, at least, their weapons won't stop Firepos, the Flame Bird.

I circle in the air, hovering out of range. Gulkien covers the crest of the hill in long strides. General Gor has leapt from his stallion and the horse rears with a snort unlike any a horse could give. So the horse-Beast lives as well! We saw the Dragon Warrior washed away with the evil Beast, but they have survived. And now, Varlot transforms. His hooves swell, and muscles ripple under a coat that hardens into armoured scales. Varlot rears onto his hind legs and towers over the soldiers. With bronze hooves planted on the ground, his arms wheel, hooves morphing into fists.

I see now that the soldiers have placed a row of logs, sharpened to deadly spikes, in front of their lines. Fools! Do they think they can stop Gulkien? The wolf charges through the hail of arrows with his girl Rider crouched *close to his fur. Her cloak ripples around her.*

Just when it looks like Gulkien will be speared, he leaps into the air. The great wings of cartilage and flesh burst from his back and he sails over the ranks, smashing into Varlot. The horse-Beast staggers backwards over a swathe of soldiers, crushing the life from them.

Tanner gives a battle cry. It is time to join this fight.

Firepos dipped her beak and swooped back towards the enemy lines. Only a few of the archers had kept in their ranks; they'd leapt apart as Gulkien had smashed into their armoured bodies, his clawed wings raking across them. Gwen was still on his back as the wolf rushed at a clutch of soldiers, seizing one in his teeth and throwing him aside with a jerk of his head. Gwen leant across his body, slicing her rapier between chinks of armour.

'Give my brother back!' Tanner heard her cry. He swooped low on Firepos, closing in on Gor who held Geffen by the scruff of his neck.

Gor roared with laughter, the sound muffled from behind his helmet. 'You thought you'd defeated me, didn't you, boy? It will take more than a swim in a river to kill me and my Beast. Ha! You didn't even manage to destroy all my soldiers. And besides, many are flocking to Derthsin's banner. Recruits are not difficult to find. You'll have to try harder.'

Anger burned in Tanner, but he tried to keep his voice steady. 'I won't let you win, Gor. I'll break you, and your foul master!' Firepos swooped over Gor and tried to claw him, but he stepped neatly aside.

Tanner guided Firepos in a low pass over the soldiers. He saw the tall, black-clad warrior making his way hurriedly between the rows of his men. He was half-dragging Geffen alongside him. In his spare hand he clutched the portion of the mask.

Arriving before a squadron of men, Gor threw

Geffen down. The boy sprawled in the dirt at the feet of a soldier. The soldier's varkule snapped viciously.

'Carry him to Vendrake's chariot. He'll take the boy to the mines. And learn to control your varkule, or you'll die!' Gor drew a finger from one ear to another, miming a slit throat.

Firepos dropped a few more feet, raking her talons through the soldiers, felling several in a chaos of howls. Just ahead were a dozen riders on the giant, hyena-like varkules. At times, they struggled to control the animals they rode. *Novices*, Tanner thought.

The varkules – each of them as tall as a horse – had a stripe of thick fur running down their spines, and sharp tusks protruding from their mouths. Tanner already knew how vicious they could be. Firepos headed straight for them, and Tanner saw the glow of a fireball growing between her talons.

'No, Firepos!' he shouted over the gusts of

wind. 'We have to stop Gor!'

Firepos climbed again, but as she did so, Tanner heard a whoop of triumph below, and the Flame Bird swerved in the air, screeching angrily. He looked back, thinking his Beast must have been wounded, but what he saw almost made him lose his grip on Firepos's feathers.

One of Gor's soldier's, an ugly brute whose face was crisscrossed with scars, was reaching, hand over hand, crawling along Firepos's back. He had a dagger clutched in one hand and grinned through rotting blackened teeth. The Flame Bird rocked from side to side, trying to throw off the unwelcome rider, but the soldier clung on, then lunged at Tanner.

Gripping Firepos with his knees, Tanner caught the soldier's wrist, stopping the plunging dagger a hand's width from his face. The soldier put his other hand behind the dagger, and pushed with all his might, forcing Tanner back against Firepos's neck. With both hands, the soldier was pressing the knife closer all the time. The tip hovered over Tanner's eye.

'You'll die or I'll take my own life,' spat the man.

Tanner sank his teeth into the soldier's wrist until he tasted blood. The soldier screamed in pain and dropped the knife. It skittered off Firepos's feathers and into empty space. Tanner managed to draw his sword. He could feel Firepos flying straight and true beneath them, trying not to jerk Tanner. The soldier leapt at him, twisting his body to avoid the blade. But Tanner lunged and pushed the sword through his enemy. He pulled the blade free, watching the steam already rising from the man's body. Blood bubbled over the soldier's twisted lips. Then his neck went limp. Tanner pushed the dead man off Firepos and watched him plummet to the ground.

Another life lost – at Tanner's own hands. Firepos let out a shrill cry. Tanner knew what she was telling him. *You must be strong.* But guilt plunged through him as he looked at his blood-stained sword. A few days ago he'd been a baker's boy. Now, he was forced to killed people.

Are we doing the right thing, Firepos? he thought.

Believe in yourself, came the answering message from his Flame Bird. Tanner knew she was right. Firepos would never have accompanied him to Foreton in the first place if they weren't following the right path. He ruffled his hands in her shimmering feathers. Even if he no longer had Grandmother Esme, at least he had his Beast.

He righted himself on Firepos's back and saw they were flying to one side of the battle below. He took in the scene quickly. Geffen was being pushed into a covered chariot, which was harnessed to a vulture with plaited leather ropes. The chariot's sides were panelled with blood-red embossed leather and instead of wheels it had ornate wooden wings protruding from either side, ready to slice through the air. The creature pulling it was spreading jet-black wings, its bald head swivelling on a long neck.

Gulkien and Varlot were rolling across the ground, tangled tooth and claw, while a wide circle of soldiers watched. Tanner panicked as he looked for Gwen. Where was she? *There!* His fellow Rider was pressed on three sides by Gor's soldiers. Gor was marching quickly to reach her, his wicked sword gripped at his side. She held her rapier, its wolf-engraved hilt tight in her hand. In the other hand she held a short axe, spinning and lunging to deflect attackers and hacking to run them through. Tanner could see she wouldn't last long against such numbers. If he didn't reach her soon, she would die.

Gulkien is locked in battle with Varlot, old foes at war. The wolf turns his shaggy head and howls towards me. He fears for his Rider. I screech back, making the soldiers clutch their ears: I will not let you down, my friend. Heat ripples through my belly and across my feathers.

I will bring my fire.

We swoop upon the soldiers surrounding Gwen. Even now, facing so many, she fights with a strange calm. Her face shows no fear, only spirit and concentration. The flames that surge from my talons bathe her face in orange light. She manages a smile as the soldiers scream. Some fall where they stand, turning to ash; others run, crying out as my flames lick over them.

Tanner turned Firepos after one pass. Most of the soldiers scattered, terrified of being burnt alive. But three spearmen remained, surrounding Gwen. The tips of their spears were levelled at her. One lunged forwards, but Gwen ducked the point, and counterattacked, sliding her sword along the shaft and into the soldier's neck. He fell before he could utter a sound.

Tanner pointed to the closest spearman and concentrated his vision on the glinting of eyes that shone from the slit in the man's helmet.

Him first. He sent the message down his body

to Firepos and felt an answering energy rise up from his Beast's feathers. They were agreed. The Flame Bird hurled a fireball, which exploded on the ground beside the approaching soldier, coating him in a wall of flame.

'Gwen!' Tanner shouted, leaning sideways and holding out an arm.

She looked up as he passed over and reached for his arm. Their fingers closed on each other, and with a grunt, he heaved her from the ground.

'Get back here, you peasants!' shouted Gor, swiping his blade through the air.

Firepos climbed, tilting her body to help Gwen scramble up behind Tanner.

'Thanks!' she said. 'Where's Geffen?'

'He's back there,' Tanner said, pointing. 'It looks like Gor's planning to take him somewhere.'

'We have to rescue him,' said Gwen.

'What about Gulkien?' asked Tanner.

The wolf was still fighting Varlot. He crouched

low to the ground in front of the horse-Beast and snarled, swiping huge claws across Varlot's armoured body. The evil Beast raised a hoof and brought it crashing down, tearing the fur from Gulkien's side.

A patch of flesh shone through, though not as red as the blood that dripped from Varlot's heaving chest. Both Beasts were injured. The horse-Beast's heavy breath misted the air. But the soldiers around were closing in. They sensed that Gulkien was weakening.

'Gulkien!' shouted Gwen. 'There'll be another time. Get away!'

The wolf lifted his head to her, eyes narrowed to slits. With a howl, he sprang off the ground and spread his wings, flying up towards them. The wound in his side was already healing over, the fur growing back. *He can heal himself just like Firepos!* Tanner realised.

When Gulkien was just below, Gwen slipped her hand from Tanner's waist and vaulted off the side of Firepos, landing neatly on the wolf's back. She rubbed her hand in his thick fur. 'Let's find my brother!' she shouted.

The Riders watch Geffen being taken to the chariot

Chapter Three

Turning from Gor's army, Tanner and Gwen's Beasts wheeled about in the air. They weren't the only creatures in the sky. Flying away from the battlefield, and almost a dot at such a distance, was the vulture-drawn chariot. 'I saw Geffen being thrown into that chariot!' Tanner shouted.

He placed the Looking Crystal to his eye and brought the chariot into close view. The scraggly-necked vulture had a wingspan of twenty paces across. It heaved its wings up and down in a slow, steady rhythm and when it looked round, almost straight at Tanner, its eyes shone with red light. Pieces of rotten flesh dangled from its beak and talons.

Gwen, flying just below, shouted for Gulkien to hurry, and the wolf surged ahead. Firepos gave chase, screeching with determination.

'We're making ground!' shouted Tanner.

The dot grew to be a shape he could see without

the Crystal, and Tanner felt a shiver of fear. Whoever was fleeing didn't seem scared that two Beasts were close in pursuit. They were climbing gradually, up through the layers of cloud and into colder air.

Tanner looked past Firepos's flaming wings to Gwen. Her face was set hard, and Gulkien bared his teeth. While they were in the air, they couldn't attack without endangering Geffen.

'Let's fly on either side of it,' Tanner yelled, 'and force them to land.'

Gwen nodded and split away on Gulkien, taking the wolf around the far side of the chariot. They closed to within twenty paces.

'Geffen!' Gwen called.

'Gwen?' came a wail from beneath the canvas covering the chariot.

'Let my brother go!' Gwen shouted. She steered Gulkien closer, and he rolled, buffeting the chariot to one side with a mighty thud. The vulture turned his bald head and brought his neck back, then spat a stream of liquid at Gulkien. The wolf howled loudly in pain and pulled away.

'It's some sort of acid,' Gwen cried to Tanner.

There was a noise and the cover of the chariot folded back. Geffen was seated, watching them. A figure dressed in a black cloak stood beside the boy. A hood covered his head, but Tanner caught a glimpse of bone-white skin beneath. Despite the lashing wind and rocking chariot, he kept a perfect balance, his shoulders back and head erect. His body was encased in an outfit of smooth, black leather, sewn together with silver thread. Long fingers clutched a staff and glowing eyes narrowed as the face turned. *It must be Vendrake!* The man Tanner had heard Gor mention.

Tanner felt his chest tighten. A long, tapering scar ran down the man's face. It pulled at the corner of his lip, curling his mouth in a permanent sneer. The edges of the scar were ragged and twisted the man's face so that it was hard to read his expression. He smiled crookedly, clearly enjoying Tanner's shock. He raised a slender hand to his face.

'This is what happens to people who cross Derthsin,' the man called. 'Now I fight for him.'

Tanner forced himself not to look away as the man leant back his head, to reveal the soft skin of his throat. The scar continued down over his neck, twisting across his skin like an angry, writhing snake. *What type of weapon does that?* Tanner wondered. And how had the man survived?

He watched Tanner from beneath hooded eyelids. Firepos gave a warning caw.

'Who are you?' called Gwen, breaking the spell.

'Derthsin's servant,' the man called. 'That's all you need to know.' There was a sudden flurry of wind that sent Firepos banking to one side. The vulture flapped its wings, sending out a stench of rotting flesh that made Tanner gag.

'Release Geffen!' he shouted, recovering himself.

The man smiled, and the remains of his lips

parted over jagged teeth. He stood taller in the chariot and raised a hand, face-out, towards Tanner. On the palm was branded the shape of a dagger's hilt. Then the man gave a tug on his sleeve and a dagger slipped down, the hilt coming to rest in his open palm – right over the branded outline. In one rapid movement, his fingers closed around the hilt, he drew a hand back over his shoulder and with a *whoosh* he released the dagger, sending it flying through the air towards Tanner, who ducked down over Firepos's feathers.

'An enemy of Derthsin's is an enemy of mine!' the man cried. The vulture squawked and brought the chariot closer to Firepos, so that the Flame Beast had to swerve out of the way. Tanner nearly fell from his Beast's shoulders, but just managed to grasp her feathers in time.

'Tanner!' Gwen cried.

Gulkien latched his claws onto the back of the flying chariot, shaking it violently from side to side, and snapping his jaws at the man. The wolf reared away with a snarl, taking splinters of the chariot in his claws, and letting them drop. Geffen was thrown against the hooded figure with a wail.

'You fool!' bellowed the man. He slapped Geffen across the cheek with the back of his hand, sending the boy sprawling into the bottom of the chariot.

'Don't you dare hurt him!' cried Gwen, her hand reaching for the rapier hidden in her cloak. Her white-blonde plaits streamed out behind her. Gulkien lunged forwards again, but the man lifted his hand towards Firepos. Another dagger slid out of his sleeve. His fingers gripped the hilt and he flicked his wrist, sending the blade arcing out.

The Flame Bird swerved out of the way of the flashing blade and it fell, twisting through the air towards the ground below. She rolled over the top of the chariot and slammed into Gulkien and Gwen. Tanner smelt the wolf's warm fur and heard his Rider scream, before he was thrown out of his seat on Firepos's back. He scrambled for a grip as he slipped down the Flame Bird's neck, and managed to close a hand on a clump of feathers. But he was hanging over the side, legs kicking empty air.

'Firepos!' he shouted. 'Help me!'

Above them, Tanner could see that the servant still had a hand trained on Firepos. There was no dagger now, but his fingers trembled. Crackling fire was pouring out of him, directed towards Tanner's Beast. *What's he doing?* The Flame Bird's eyes had rolled back in her head and she was losing height, wings dangling uselessly, going into a dive. Shreds of cloud whipped past as Tanner struggled to pull himself to safety. He heaved himself up among Firepos's glowing feathers and looked over his shoulder at the patches of fields spinning below. They were plummeting towards them. Gulkien and Gwen were nowhere to be seen.

Tanner heaved himself back up to Firepos's neck, and tried to pull her head. She didn't respond. The ground was approaching fast. He leant close to the Flame Bird's ear, with the wind buffeting his face. 'Firepos,' he said. 'Wake up! Please!' Now he was close enough to see the wind making swirling patterns in the field's long grass below. Tanner drew a breath, bracing himself for impact.

'Firepos!'

I am weightless; I feel nothing. Then Tanner's voice penetrates the silence. He calls my name. It is my duty to respond.

My vision returns and blurs and I see the earth. It drags at my body, pulling me down. I circle towards the ground, wings whipping back. No! I am suddenly awake and with a flood of strength, my muscles become alert and I beat them fast and strong. A surge upwards. Then another wing beat…

But I am falling too quickly.

My talons take the impact and we crash into the ground. For a moment, all is white, blinding. One wing is folded beneath me, the other beats the ground uselessly.

The man of evil in the chariot channels Derthsin's power. Does that explain why I am so weak?

I see my Rider, lying beside me on the grass. Blood leaks from a wound on his head, but he stirs. I crawl towards him, sending out a call. His hand reaches up and rests upon my beak.

I am here, Chosen Rider.

Gulkien alights beside us. His closing wings flatten the grass, and the girl Rider springs off his back, dropping to Tanner's side. Our friends, returned to us.

'Tanner!'

He opened his eyes and saw Gwen. The grass was soft beneath him, but his head was pounding. 'Firepos?' he muttered.

The Flame Bird cawed, a comforting sound. Tanner managed to sit up with Gwen's help, and reached for his head, drawing his fingers back wet with blood.

'Careful,' said Gwen. 'Take it slowly.'

Tanner's mind cleared. 'What about your brother?'

Gwen's eyes moistened for a moment, but she blinked the tears away. 'When I saw you falling, I couldn't just leave you… He was carried away in the chariot.' She shuddered. 'I've never seen a man like that. He's worse than Gor.'

'I know what you mean.' Tanner tested his legs. Nothing seemed broken. 'With Gor, at least we can understand what he is – a general who follows orders. But that servant… He has a strong connection with Derthsin. Did you see what he did to Firepos?'

How had that happened to his Beast? How could she plunge from the skies like a dead weight? But he pushed these thoughts away. Gwen had lost her brother. Through half-closed eyes he studied his friend. Her plaits were bedraggled and dark shadows stained the skin beneath her eyes. She looked exhausted. 'I'm sorry we couldn't get your brother back,' he said.

Gwen shook her head. Her face coloured as she looked at the ground. 'You were right,' she said in a quiet voice. 'He did betray us, stealing away in the night like that.' She frowned. 'But how was he able to let Gor know where we were?'

Tanner sighed. 'I think Gor let him escape, when I fought them in the mountains. He must have already given Geffen instructions for what to do if they were ever parted. It was only a matter of time until the general found us.' He cleared his throat. 'Geffen saw the map, didn't he? He'll be able to tell Vendrake where the next piece of the mask is. And he'll tell Derthsin. We have to get to the mines before they do.'

Firepos climbed to her feet, clawing the ground and flexing her wings, casting Tanner and Gwen in shadow. Her feathers rippled with colour, from amber to vermillion.

'Are you ready?' asked Tanner. Gwen was staring at the ground. Two red spots had appeared on her cheeks. 'Gwen? What's wrong?'

She looked up at him. 'If Geffen wants to share secrets, he won't just be leading Vendrake to the mines. He'll know exactly where the mask is. Jonas used to tell us stories about the eastern tunnels and a treasure buried there.'

Tanner felt the energy drain from him. 'Why did you never share this with me before?' He tried to keep any accusation out of his voice; he knew Gwen had done a lot to help him.

She shrugged, but there was nothing careless in her movement. She looked loaded down with the cares of the world. 'Jonas was very special to Geffen and I. We don't often talk about him. The day he left...' She turned her face away so that Tanner couldn't see the tears he knew would be brimming in her eyes. He waited for her to compose herself, for her breathing to calm down again. Gulkien watched her keenly.

Eventually, she looked back round. 'I'm sorry. I don't know why I didn't say anything before.'

'Well, you've told me now. That's the main thing. It's not too late. Come on.' He smiled at Gwen. He wanted her to find her spirit again. 'I know you're a good fighter. We just need to get to the mines.'

Gwen flicked back her cloak to reveal her throwing axes. 'I'm an *excellent* fighter,' she said, smiling.

Tanner grinned back. 'Has he always been jealous of you?' he asked, as he watched Gwen unroll the map. He didn't have to say Geffen's name – he knew Gwen would understand.

'I don't know,' she said. She released the gauze from her locket, spreading it over the details penned across the scroll. 'He wouldn't have been happy if he'd known that Jonas had given the secrets of the map to me alone. Yes… He's always been competitive, wanting to be the best. Perhaps it isn't jealousy, exactly.'

'Perhaps not,' Tanner said quietly, 'but being competitive shouldn't mean you lead your sister to near-death.'

Gwen shook her head. 'Can we stop talking about it?' She looked up into Tanner's face. 'Please.'

Tanner crouched beside her, the parchment on the ground between them. It was more like soft cloth than paper. The secret gauze transformed the map into something much more special. As she straightened it over the top, the surface moved like water under the shifting clouds showing the entire kingdom. Four points began to glow like gemstones – the pieces of the Mask of Death.

'We're here,' said Gwen, pointing to the section of rolling plains in the centre of the kingdom. 'Vendrake was heading north.' She indicated the glowing portion of mask in the mountains at the far reaches of the map. 'We're right. Geffen must be taking him to the mines.'

Tanner leapt up and rushed to Firepos. The

Flame Bird lowered herself to the ground, and he climbed up, using the crook of her wing as a foothold.

'We have to hurry,' he said. 'Gor will be marching his army that way too.'

Gwen rolled up the map and put away the magical gauze. She gripped the fur of Gulkien's neck and hoisted herself onto his back.

'To the Northern Mountains!' Tanner shouted.

Soaring over Avantia

Chapter Four

Tanner watched the treetops grow smaller below them as Firepos pounded her wings, picking up speed. Gulkien flew beside them, the air rippling his fur. They soared over flat, empty fields. Tanner spotted stone ruins, overgrown with trees and high grass, and just beyond it, a little village. The thatched houses spread unevenly out from a stone manor at the centre.

Further on, a line of trees marked a boundary to another network of wheat fields surrounding a river town, ringed with a wooden wall. The hills around it shimmered with grass and stands of trees, but Tanner could see the discoloured lines and jags of weather-eaten stone where older roads and proud houses had once stood. Another village was built on a hillside that was topped with crumbling brick. The boundaries changed, but Avantia's people remained.

For now, Tanner thought.

Gwen hunched low on Gulkien's back, peering over his shoulders to gaze down at the passing fields. They approached what looked like a trade route – a beaten dirt path marked at the edges with black distance-stones.

Tanner tried to ignore the dread in his stomach. Somewhere out there was Derthsin. And through Vendrake, he seemed to have a terrible hold over Firepos.

The Beasts ducked lower in the sky. The deserted trade route had led them to sprawling black rubble. Blocky ruins clustered inside scorched fields. The houses had been gutted to crumbled corners and empty door frames, and a large building in the centre of the village, which Tanner guessed might have been a great hall or a market place, had been burnt to the ground, leaving only the jagged edges and a haunting brick chimney. He couldn't see anything moving, and the roads were empty in every direction.

'This is what the whole kingdom will become

if we don't stop Derthsin,' Tanner called over the whistling wind to Gwen. She drew her cloak tighter around her body and nodded grimly, holding on to Gulkien's fur with one hand.

They swept on over the plains until in the distance they saw slate-gray stone.

'Look!' Gwen cried out. 'The Northern Mountains!'

Ahead, Tanner saw sharp peaks, topped with snow and ringed with low-hanging clouds. They flew in silence for a long time, following the steep hills up into the mountains.

Firepos and Gulkien slowed as they neared the outskirts of a town, perched in a gap between the steep slopes. Even without the help of the Looking Crystal, Tanner could see people moving among the buildings.

The wolf turned his head to Firepos and growled, a low rumble like distant thunder. Tanner's Beast called back, and both creatures adjusted their paths and glided downwards.

'Hey!' said Tanner. 'Did you ask them to do that?'

Gwen shook her head, frowning. Why had the Beasts decided it was time to land? Tanner clung on as Firepos descended towards the hilltop town.

'Castor! Castor! Castor!'

Chapter Five

Gulkien has sensed it too. This place is special.

It draws us, like the moon pulling at the tides. Through a rush of air, I clamp my talons onto bare rock. Gulkien hits the ground at a run, his leathery wings folding into his back in a clatter of dry joints and sinew.

He snarls with bared fangs, excitement ruffling his thick fur.

Be calm, my brother. The one who waits here knows we are coming. She will be ready for us.

'Why are we landing here?' Gwen asked, slipping down from Gulkien's back and taking out the map. 'The piece of the mask is half a day's walk away according to this.'

'The Beasts must know something we don't,' Tanner said, climbing off Firepos's wing. They had to get to the mask before Vendrake and Gor, but... *Firepos can't have brought us here without a very good reason*, he thought.

Gwen held the map in front of her, peering at the surface.

'Colton,' she said at last. 'We're at a town called Colton.'

'We should leave Gulkien and Firepos here,' said Tanner. 'If people spot two Beasts they haven't seen before, they're sure to get jittery – and hostile.'

Gwen stroked her Beast's fur and he gave a soft growl, pawing the dried earth. 'He's right,' she said. 'You two have to hide. But don't go too far – we don't know what we're going to find. Do you understand?'

Gulkien's wings sprang from his back once more, and he stretched them, then licked his sharp teeth, ran a few paces and leapt into the air. The wolf curled his hind legs tightly under him and beat his wings powerfully.

Firepos cocked her head and launched into the air, the swoop of her wings nearly knocking Tanner off-balance. As she rose higher, she circled and went after the wolf, her feathers shimmering.

When Gulkien howled, Firepos sent out a returning cry, and they flew together into a patch of low clouds hanging over the town.

'Looks like they spotted the best place to hide,' smiled Gwen.

Tanner grinned back. 'Now let's find out why they brought us here.'

Tanner jumped from boulder to boulder as they approached Colton, leaping over deep fissures in the ground.

They scrambled across a cluster of rocks and found themselves on a dirt road leading to the village. It was churned with hoof-prints and wheel tracks. Tanner knelt to examine them.

'These tracks are too narrow to be from farm carts,' he said. 'They've been made by army chariots.'

Tanner ran his fingers through the beaten dirt

and grass. Dark streaks flecked the grass: dried blood.

'I don't understand,' said Gwen. 'Gor's troops can't have come this far already. Most of the soldiers were on foot.'

'Perhaps Derthsin has more than one army,' said Tanner grimly.

The mountain levelled as they picked their way along the road. When they reached the edge of the town they stopped, and stared about them in shock. The roofs of houses had been burnt away, leaving deep rings scorched onto the half-ruined walls. Splintered boards and bricks cluttered the blackened streets, and Tanner could see gashes and deep holes in the sides of the crumbling walls, made by swords and arrows.

They passed through the ruined town gate. It was clear that there'd been an attempt to repair it, but the posts still leant dangerously. Ahead, a group of ragged townspeople were using lengths of rope to hoist a long wooden beam onto a broken rooftop. As the adults worked, children chased each other between piles of broken street debris. This town had been attacked. It was trying to put itself right, but Tanner could see that the devastation had been massive.

'Higher!' a woman on the roof called. She reached for the beam as other women pulled a rope to raise it. 'Steady!' The woman caught the beam in both hands. As she guided it onto the roof, she saw Tanner and Gwen – and froze.

The other townspeople turned. The children stopped working.

Tanner raised his hand in greeting, but the townspeople only stared back. Their faces were tired, their eyes empty. Tanner glanced from one woman's torn skirt to a girl's ragged pigtail, then looked back at the woman struggling with the beam. *They're all…*

'Women and children,' Gwen murmured.

The people whispered and continued to stare suspiciously as Tanner and Gwen kept walking.

Some of the women clutched the children tightly as they passed. At the next corner, a stooped old man was nailing a new board onto a shattered doorframe. The hammer shook in his gnarled hands. More children collected smashed slivers of pottery and twisted nails from the dirt.

'This is horrible,' Gwen said. 'Everything in this village – the houses, the streets…'

They stopped when they saw a fragile, elderly woman crawling through a patch of black dirt, picking vegetables. Her garden had been flattened and crushed by horses and soldiers' boots, and was cluttered with burnt wood and brick shards. The woman found a shrivelled carrot in the mess and as Tanner watched her pick through the rubble for bruised, half-smashed potatoes, hot anger welled in his chest.

Gwen ran over to the old woman and knelt beside her. 'Please,' she said, 'can I help you fill your vegetable basket?'

But the woman scrambled away, startled.

'Who are you?' she said, glancing between Gwen and Tanner. 'What do you want? I don't have anything! They burnt my home, everything that was mine!'

'We're here to help you,' Tanner said, as gently as he could. The old woman made him think of Grandmother Esme – her house ransacked, her broken body left for dead by Derthsin's troops. He glanced at the scrap of red linen tied around his wrist, the only memento he had left of the woman who had brought him up. It was grubby and frayed now – how much longer would it survive intact?

'Help?' the woman repeated. Her hands trembled as she offered them the withered carrots and potatoes. 'Here, take them. Take anything you want. Just please don't hurt me.' She cowered to the ground.

Tanner and Gwen stared at each other with horror.

'Derthsin's army came to our villages too,' said

Tanner. He could hear other people murmuring to each other from behind his back. He raised his voice so that they could hear. 'My grandmother and everyone else I knew were slaughtered…'

He stopped as the old woman seized his arm. 'They took my grandson, Corrin,' she said. 'The soldiers came in the night, ten days ago. They went through every house, pulling the men outside, out of the arms of their wives and mothers…' Her face contorted with pain at the memory. 'They killed the men. We buried them in the field outside the town wall. But the boys… The soldiers lined up all the boys they could find old enough to work and put ropes around their necks. One woman tried to save her son, but the soldiers beat her. Then they took them away…'

Gwen put her arm round the woman's shoulders as she sobbed.

A sudden shout drew Tanner's attention. They left the old woman, passing through the crowd and past more ruined blocks, until they approached the town square. Women and children had gathered in a great circle. They were chanting, 'Castor! Castor! Castor!'

Tanner and Gwen pushed their way through until they could see what was happening. In the middle of the square, a boy of about Tanner's age was waving a sword and grinning at the crowd. His hair hung in golden locks, framing his face, and an easy smile lit up his eyes. He had the wide shoulders and muscular arms of someone who practised hard with his sword. Tanner noticed a dagger sheathed in his belt. It wasn't hidden, like Gwen's throwing axes. *He wants people to know he can fight*, thought Tanner.

The boy strutted in a slow circle and thumped his chest to encourage the chanting. He tossed his sword into the air and, as it spun, he clapped in time with the chants – 'Castor, Castor!' – then caught the sword behind his back.

'So, who's next?' the boy shouted. He pretended to fumble with his sword and laughed. 'See, I'm not a great swordsman!' He spun the blade in a fast double-swipe. 'Which of you thinks he can face me? Step in now, and I'll fight you with one hand behind my back!'

The way Castor smirked at the crowd, as they cheered and encouraged him, made Tanner clench his jaw with irritation. Gwen nudged him with her elbow.

'He's quite a showman, isn't he?' she said, raising her voice over the noise.

Tanner scowled. 'Show-off, more like. We're wasting our time. I don't want to watch this preening fool.'

But to his surprise, Gwen was smiling.

'He's good!' she called over the noise.

Tanner stared at her. 'Good?' he said. 'Are you out of your mind? Look at him!'

'Oh, I know,' she said, 'you were right when you called him a show-off. But do you see how fast he is with his sword? I've never seen anyone fight like that.'

Back in the circle, Castor spread his arms wide. 'What, no one here's brave enough? Everyone's terrified of me? I don't blame you – I would be too!'

A voice piped up. 'I'll fight you!'

Tanner peered over to see who the challenger was. A thin boy who couldn't have been older than eight or nine stepped into the circle. The crowd whooped and cheered as the boy raised his weapon – not a sword, but a poker.

Castor rolled his eyes. 'No, no, no,' he said. 'You're lost, little boy. I am *Castor*. Do you hear me? You can't fight me!'

'I c-can,' the boy said.

'What?' said Castor. 'Speak up – they can't hear you!'

'Y-yes, I can,' the boy stammered. The poker trembled in his hand, but he stood up straight to face Castor. 'On Midsummer Eve, my father was killed when they took my brothers.'

Midsummer Eve! That was several dawns ago – more than Tanner could remember.

He exchanged a glance with Gwen. That meant that Derthsin's armies had been attacking dwellings even before their homes were ransacked. How long had this been going on for? Tanner had no way of knowing – few people moved between the towns and villages of Avantia. Word travelled slowly. But now one thing was clear: Grandmother Esme had not been the first to die.

Castor frowned. 'So? Did you get hit on the head and lose your brains? Step out of the circle, boy.'

The Northern Mountains loomed over the town, jagged and dark in the daylight. The air was tense, as if a storm was nearby, ready to break.

'No,' the boy said. 'When they took my father away, he told me I was the man in my family. I'm going to fight you to prove that I'm a man.' His bottom lip trembled and, for a moment, Tanner had to turn his face away.

Castor didn't waste time on pity. He knocked the boy's poker up, and twisted his blade in an arc that sent the boy's weapon spinning away. It hit the dusty ground.

'I'm going to put a stop to this!' Tanner said, setting off towards the outside of the circle, with Gwen at his side.

The boy was shaking, watching Castor's sword. 'Wait…' he said.

But Castor swung his blade high. The boy ducked, and Castor shoved him to the ground, planting a boot on the boy's chest. He lowered the tip of his sword to the boy's throat.

The crowd broke out into fresh cheers.

Castor grinned, showing white teeth, and waved his arm theatrically over the boy. 'Go home to your mother,' he jeered. As the boy picked up his poker, Castor kicked his behind, knocking him into the crowd.

Tanner didn't need to get involved. The fight had ended without bloodshed. 'See?' he scoffed to Gwen. 'He's nothing but an arrogant coward.'

As he spoke, the crowd noise dipped, and the last word – *coward* – sounded louder than he'd intended. All faces turned to Tanner, and the darkest of all was Castor's.

Tanner meets Nera

Chapter Six

Castor flicked his sword from side to side like a pendulum as he studied Tanner. His eyes fell to Tanner's own blade.

'It looks like we have another challenger,' Castor sneered.

The spectators erupted into fresh applause.

'I don't want to fight you,' shouted Tanner over the din.

'You come here and call me a coward, yet you won't back up your words with actions,' said Castor.

'I've seen enough *fighting*, as you call it,' said Tanner. 'I know my true enemies.'

Castor gave an uneasy smile. 'All right, all right,' he said, signalling at the crowd to quieten down. 'It's getting late. We've been here all day, and my new friend is probably tired. The challenges are over until tomorrow…'

But the crowd groaned with disappointment

and began to chant again. 'Castor! Castor!'

Castor shrugged. 'What's your name, stranger?'

'Tanner,' he said.

He eyed Tanner with amusement.

'Tanner...' he repeated, smiling. 'You look familiar. Yes, that's it! I once owned a hog that looked just like you. I slit his throat.'

Tanner felt a surge of rage, and pushed past the jeering crowd, unsheathing his sword. Blood pounded in his ears and he could barely think straight enough to plan what he'd do next.

'You stepped into the circle, friend,' Castor said, pointing his sword at Tanner's face. 'Nobody is going to save you now. Give me your sword, and I'll let you walk away.'

'Tanner, don't...' called Gwen. But he hardly heard.

'You'll have to take it from me,' Tanner snapped back at the boy from Colton.

Castor grinned. He paced closer to Tanner, his eyes narrowed, while the crowd cheered. His spare hand drifted towards the dagger in his belt. Tanner drew his sword, and held it low, ready to protect his torso.

Castor drew his dagger and attacked. In one hand he wielded his sword, in his other, the dagger. He swiped left with the sword's blade, and when Tanner blocked, Castor spun – just like he had with the skinny young boy – and darted forwards with his dagger. Tanner stumbled backwards and Castor kicked him to the ground. Castor's sword blade was at Tanner's throat. He raised his dagger above Tanner's chest.

'All I have to do is let go,' he said, jerking his head at the dagger, 'and it will plunge into your heart.' Before he finished speaking, Tanner rolled to one side. Castor released the dagger but it pierced the ground. Tanner jumped to his feet and as Castor retrieved his dagger, Tanner brought his sword down. Castor straightened up just in time, blocking Tanner's attack. Hastily, Castor shoved his dagger into his belt and attacked again with his sword. Tanner parried high, dodged a side-swipe, and just managed to bat down Castor's sword. They circled.

He's better than I am, Tanner realised. He could see that Castor knew it too. He was waving his fist at the crowd.

Castor knocked Tanner's sword down, forcing him to double up. Tanner rolled under a swipe at his neck and dodged backwards, so that Castor hacked the dirt.

That's it, thought Tanner, as Castor, breathing heavily, wiped the dirt from his blade. *I'm a faster mover than he is – I'll tire him out!*

Tanner saw Gwen in the crowd, surrounded by shouting women and children. Her face was creased with concern. Tanner was almost caught off-guard as Castor charged at him. Tanner rolled and vaulted a low swing that almost caught his leg. He circled away again.

'Stand still!' Castor shouted, panting. 'Fight like a man!' Castor feinted right – but he was slowing down. Tanner dodged Castor's blow, knocked his sword down, and slashed at him, slicing through Castor's tunic.

He's tiring. Tanner pressed in again. Castor blocked in fluid strokes and tried to push him back. But Tanner leapt around him, and as Castor spun, Tanner caught Castor's sword from behind – the blades clanking and scraping – and Tanner pulled, trying to yank Castor's weapon away. Castor strained against him, panting, his face slick with sweat.

The roar of the crowd was deafening. They weren't just cheering Castor's name anymore – Tanner was drawing just as many cheers.

People climbed onto ruined rooftops and children perched on women's shoulders to get a better view.

His face twisted with effort, Castor yanked his sword free. He yelled a battle cry as he leapt at Tanner.

Tanner braced his feet wide, and held his sword

ready to meet Castor's. The blow made his blade shake so violently it felt as if it might shatter. But Castor had landed awkwardly. Tanner shoved him backwards, and as Castor stumbled, Tanner clashed his blade against the other boy's. Castor fell to the ground. Tanner kicked his opponent's sword away, put his boot on Castor's chest, and lowered his sword to the other boy's throat. The crowd applauded.

'This fight is over,' Tanner said, wiping the sweat from his eyes, his chest heaving. Castor stared up at him, more surprised than frightened. Tanner looked for Gwen again in the crowd, and smiled with relief when he saw her. But she was cupping her hands around her mouth, shouting something at him.

'...out!'

Tanner frowned. *Look out?*

Something hit him from behind. The world blurred as the ground came up to smack him in the face and chest. The crowd fell silent. Tanner rolled over. He saw a great, coiled ball of golden fur and muscle.

It was a massive cat, as large as Gulkien. The creature arched its back, its tail pointing straight up. Its eyes glittered with an angry green light, and it bared razor-sharp teeth at Tanner. At the edge of his vision was Castor, sitting up and brushing the dirt from his hair. The crowd screamed and scrambled away in fear.

A Beast!

Tanner stayed frozen on the ground, not daring to move. His eyes fixed on the creature, as its tense, gigantic muscles rippled under golden fur. Dagger-like claws slid out from its paws and it spat angrily at him. The Beast tensed, ready to pounce. Beyond the creature, Tanner could see Castor smiling. Tanner felt empty fear in his gut. *I'm going to die.*

Beasts in combat

Chapter Seven

'You've made Nera angry,' said Castor, wiping his sword as he walked up to where Tanner lay splayed under the Beast. 'Now you'll stay down there in the dirt until I let you up.'

With a laugh, Castor allowed Nera to wrap her tail around his waist. Then he was swung up to sit astride her neck. The Beast raked the ground next to Tanner's head, while Castor grinned and folded his arms across his chest.

Tanner looked from the Beast to Castor. *He's been chosen,* Tanner realised with a jolt, *just as Firepos chose me, and Gulkien chose Gwen. It can't be!*

I sense that my Chosen Rider is under attack – from an old friend. I break through the clouds, plummeting down on outspread wings, flames flickering at their edges. I land on the ruined market wall. I see Nera. She is wild, crazed to protect her Chosen Rider. This is not a game. Nera wants blood – I can see it in her eyes.

Her loyalty has clouded her senses. Tanner is her prey.
  I call to Gulkien. We must act – now!

Tanner started as the air rushed back in a whirlwind of dust. The crowd screamed and Firepos and Gulkien burst into the square on thundering wings. As Firepos shrieked, Gulkien howled a jolting, visceral cry. The villagers covered their ears, and the beasts swooped low, huge and angry.

Firepos flew at Nera, beating her wings and snapping her hooked beak, forcing the Beast away from Tanner. Gulkien caught Nera's leg in his jaws and yanked her into the air so that Castor lunged forward to cling to his Beast's throat. The giant cat twisted, clawing Gulkien's face in a bloody spray that knocked Gulkien off-balance, but before Nera landed, Firepos had her. She clamped her beak on Nera's neck – Nera's claws flashed at Firepos's eyes – and the Flame Bird jerked backwards, releasing her opponent.

Gulkien roared, baring his gums and fangs.

Murmurs rippled round the crowd as the people stared in astonishment at the three Beasts. 'I was told about such things by my father,' Tanner heard someone say, 'but I never thought they really existed.'

Castor leapt down from his Beast. Turning in a slow circle, he took in the sight of Firepos and Gulkien, looking them up and down. He tucked a stray lock of golden hair behind an ear and straightened his shoulders, facing up to the Beasts. Gulkien let out a low snarl.

'Your pets are impressive.' He paused. 'If you like that type of thing.' He rested a hand on Nera's thick fur and smiled up at her massive face. 'Personally, I prefer a Beast that can actually *fight*.' As he spoke the last word, Nera flexed her paw and a vast claw sprang towards Tanner as he sprawled on the ground, placing its point against his chest. He didn't dare move. Firepos cried out with an angry caw and Nera slid her claws back into the pads of her feet and pulled her paw away from Tanner.

Don't be fooled. Nera is a friend. Tanner heard Firepos's message rumble through him.

So why is his Chosen Rider acting like an enemy? he thought.

Gwen ran towards Tanner as he got to his feet. 'Are you all right?' she asked.

Before Tanner could respond, Castor threw back his head and laughed. 'This isn't over. Get on your Beast, and let's see who deserves to win!'

'Whatever you want,' Tanner shouted back. 'I'm ready!'

Stop now, Firepos pleaded with him. *End this.* Tanner wouldn't listen and pushed Firepos's message out of his head.

Gwen grabbed his arm. 'Stop it! This is stupid – you don't have to fight! Have you forgotten? We have more important things to do.'

Castor laughed again on Nera's back as she

leapt from spot to spot, covering the entire length of the square then back again, her golden coat shining.

Tanner had never seen a Beast move so fast. He struggled to contain his anger. As Castor's Beast paused, he stepped up.

The other boy raised his sword. 'Well, Tanner, get on your bird, so I can fight you properly. Beast against Beast! Or are you too much of a coward?'

Tanner's anger flared again and he found himself climbing onto Firepos, disturbing her feathers as he scrambled. *Let's end this now!* Tanner silently told his Beast.

'What about the mask?' Gwen cried. 'What about defeating Derthsin?'

'I need to wipe the grin from Castor's face first,' Tanner insisted, refusing to look at her. He drew his sword.

'You're a fool,' Castor yelled. 'This is going to be fun!'

The crowd was watching again from the nearby buildings, and when Nera bounded up to Firepos the villagers scrambled onto the broken rooftops and nearby trees to get a better look.

'Let's show him, Firepos,' Tanner said. 'Fly!'

Firepos shrieked and took off, surging high above the square. As Tanner and Firepos rose, Nera circled the ground below them, raking the air with extended talons. It almost looked as though the huge cat was smiling. Tanner realised that Castor's Beast was thinking the same as Firepos: that this was a silly skirmish they needed to get out of the way. For a moment, he felt foolish – then he spotted Castor's mocking grin, and red spots of anger danced before Tanner's eyes. Nera sent out a teasing paw towards Firepos's tail feathers and Tanner's Beast jerked awkwardly to one side. That was all the excuse Tanner needed…

I twist in the air. Nera fights well, but so do I. We understand each other – this is not so much a fight, as a game. We shall not harm each other, but these boys have so much anger running through them. They need to work it off. But I must control myself. I trust Nera to do the same. My Chosen Rider whispers into my ear, 'We will win. Help me, Firepos.'

I don't want to hurt Nera, and I won't. But Tanner's anger must run its course.

'This is your last chance!' Castor yelled. 'Surrender, or they'll be picking your pieces off the square in the morning!'

Tanner glanced beneath him. 'You're all talk!' he called down.

Castor laughed and raised his sword. 'You coward. Taking to the air, far out of reach. What kind of a fighter does that make you?'

Tanner dug his knees into Firepos's sides and directed her down. His Beast landed in the dust. Tanner and Castor locked eyes.

Castor leant on Nera to urge her on. The Beast surged towards Tanner and Firepos. Nera roared, her cry high and angry. Castor levelled his sword and bellowed.

'Now, Firepos!' Tanner told his Beast.

Firepos swooped forward so suddenly that the wind knocked Tanner backwards; he caught his balance and aimed his sword. The Beasts rushed closer – Nera roaring like thunder, Firepos screaming a terrible Flame Bird cry – and the boys braced their blades.

Tanner saw the glint in Nera's eye and the vicious curve of her fangs. Firepos suddenly broke left, and Nera darted to the right. Tanner ducked as Castor leant out dangerously far and slashed his blade through the air. The people watching cried out in alarm.

'Too late!' Tanner called back.

He heard Castor yelling impatiently at his Beast. 'Come on, Nera! Now!'

His Beast darted at Firepos. Tanner held his sword with both hands, gripping Firepos's body with his thighs. As he rushed close to Castor,

Firepos flying low to the ground, he tensed. Their blades clashed in a shower of sparks and the impact almost wrenched his shoulder out of its joint. Castor's sword sailed through the air, clattering into the square.

'You've lost!' shouted Tanner.

For the first time since Tanner had met him, Castor looked uncertain, but his face set in a grim smile. 'I've still got Nera!' he called back.

He urged the Beast round, and Firepos and Nera came at each other again. Firepos was flying so quickly that the air-rush sucked Tanner over Firepos's neck – he slipped, almost fell, but caught himself at the last moment.

A terrible howl cut through the air, and Gulkien flew into view. Gwen rushed to her Beast, her face full of understanding.

'Stop!' she called. 'The village is being attacked!'

Derthsin's warrior perishes

Chapter Eight

Gulkien calls us. A warning cry.

Nera and I break away from each other, and her Rider cries out in anger. Creatures are already swarming the market square – varkules and riders. A cry rings out from the soldiers: 'Death has come, death has come…' The people scatter, but are chased down. The varkule riders pursue them with lassos, bringing the townsfolk down like cattle, slinging them over their saddles.

I call to Nera. It is time to calm our hearts – our anger should be directed towards our true enemies, not each other. She bows her golden head in understanding.

The villagers were screaming.

'Round up the women and children!' shouted one of the soldiers. 'Any who can work. And keep your eyes peeled for those Beasts and their friends.'

Tanner saw an elderly woman squirming on the ground, her ankles bound with rope. Three varkules had pressed a clutch of Castor's people against a wall, snapping with drooling jaws. Tanner could smell their awful scent.

The foul, snarling animals didn't see Gulkien until his shadow was directly overhead. The wolf collapsed his wings and dropped. Gwen's Beast snarled and fought, tearing men apart with his claws and throwing bodies to the ground. Blood welled up from an open wound in a soldier's chest. With a mixture of ragged growls and human shouts of terror, those varkules and their riders were no more. Gwen was watching Gulkien from a distance, her face white. Then she pulled her rapier from its hiding place in her cloak's lining, ready to fight.

Tanner steered Firepos over the crowd. With two slashes of his sword, two enemy riders fell dead beside their steeds. The varkules, panicked from the aerial attack, ranged up onto their hind legs, nearly throwing their riders. They snarled at the Beasts above them, pawing the air, the hair on their spines bristling. But the Beasts were far out of reach. One by one they retreated, galloping away. One of them dragged a lifeless armoured corpse behind, tangled in its stirrups.

'Fall back!' shouted the soldiers' leader. 'Retreat!'

His men responded, charging from the village through any road they could find. The leader wasn't so lucky. Nera pounced from the top of a building, burying her claws in his varkule's chest. The hyena-like creature rolled over its rider, the striped fur on its spine crushed beneath its weight. An ear hung, torn and bloody, from the varkule's head. The animal gave an anguished wail as its rider lay crumpled beneath it. Tanner could see the awkward twist of the man's legs and the way that his head hung at an angle – he would fight no more.

As the square emptied of attackers, Tanner guided Firepos down beside Nera and Gulkien. He jumped off and sheathed his sword, taking a slow breath. The crowd watched.

'I've never seen the like!' an old woman said.

Castor looked at the enemy's dead leader, his face pale. His eyes shifted to Tanner uncertainly. Tanner's guilt returned, pulsing through him. There was no ignoring it now.

'I'm sorry. You and I are not supposed to fight,' Tanner said to Castor. 'The Riders of the Beasts must work together against things like this happening. We have to stop the warlord, Derthsin.'

Castor burst into laughter. 'Work with you? You must be joking!'

'Listen to Tanner,' Gwen told Castor. She was sheathing her rapier back in her cloak; Castor watched with wide eyes. 'Derthsin is nothing but hate and evil, and if he succeeds, no one will be safe. He'll use the Mask of Death to control the Beasts – including Nera. He'll wreak havoc through Avantia.'

Nera growled and pressed her nose into Gulkien's fur as if they were old friends.

'Maybe,' Castor said. He took out a cloth and began to clean his sword blade. 'But have you seen Derthsin's army? They have already been here once. This is just a tiny section of the men. His soldiers are trained killers.'

Tanner noticed that Castor's hand was trembling. 'If we don't stop Derthsin, no one will,' he said.

'You can't even beat *me*,' said Castor. 'What makes you think you can beat Derthsin?' Castor's bravado had returned, but Tanner wasn't convinced.

'I did beat you, remember,' Tanner said evenly.

'A lucky shot…' Castor began.

'Will you both *stop*?' said Gwen. Firepos screeched and Gulkien snarled impatiently.

But Tanner's pulse was quickening again. 'Derthsin's soldiers killed my grandmother. They…'

'That's a shame,' Castor said, and he turned away. 'But grandmothers die all the time, my friend…'

Tanner lunged forwards with an ugly cry and tackled Castor from behind. They both went down in a cloud of dust. Castor rolled over, and Tanner punched him in the stomach, until Castor kicked Tanner away and rolled free. They both stood, panting and filthy with dirt.

Tanner's lip was bleeding. 'Don't you care about anyone but yourself? Castor, your own people were captured – doesn't that matter to you?'

Castor shifted uncomfortably, and when he spoke his voice was quieter than before. 'Of course I care.'

'You were chosen by a Beast,' Tanner said. 'Nera picked you. Out of everyone she picked you, just like our Beasts chose us.'

'Yes,' Castor said.

Gwen brightened. 'Think about what we can achieve together,' she said.

Firepos called to Nera. Gulkien stepped forward and barked a greeting, his fur bristling, leathery wings protruding. The three Beasts circled each other. Nera threw back her head and gave an eerie yowl, a terrible blast of noise that shook the ruined buildings and made the ground tremble. The hint of a smile passed Castor's lips as he watched the Beasts together.

'I still don't understand,' Tanner said. 'Why are you here, Castor? Why didn't Derthsin's men take you with the rest of the boys?'

'Why wasn't *I* taken?' Castor said, thrusting out his chest. 'I pick my fights, and I enter battle when *I* decide.'

'What does that mean?' Gwen asked, frowning.

'It means I'm smart,' Castor said. But Tanner noticed the way that his eyes fell to the ground; he couldn't hold Gwen's gaze. 'That's why they didn't get me – anyway, we have to get moving if we're going to save the others.'

'So you're coming with us?' Gwen asked. Castor nonchalantly shrugged his shoulders.

Tanner said, 'Do you know where they took the boys?'

'The soldiers led them away in lines, tied together. They're slaves now.'

'Slaves?' Gwen said. 'What for?'

'This one's alive!' cried a female voice.

Tanner and the others turned. A woman was standing beside the sprawled body of a varkule. Beneath its body, Tanner saw a set of legs. He ran over with Gwen.

The varkule rider looked up at them from beneath his dead mount. One side of his face was matted with blood and his chest rose and fell in shallow breaths.

Tanner heard a movement behind him, and Castor leapt on top of the varkule. He pulled out his dagger, ready to stab the man. Tanner pushed him backwards. 'No!'

'Let me kill him!' said Castor. As Tanner held a hand against his chest, he leant in to whisper to Castor. 'He might be able to tell us something.'

Castor lowered the dagger and nodded, rubbing his eyes with the back of his sleeve. He shoved the dagger back down the side of his boot.

Tanner returned to the injured soldier and knelt beside him, bringing his face close to the man's bloodied ear.

'Who sent you?' he said. 'Was it Derthsin?'

The soldier grimaced. 'Don't be a fool!' he croaked. 'Derthsin died years ago!'

Tanner shared a look with Gwen. They both knew that Derthsin was somehow still alive.

'Then who do you work for?' Gwene snapped.

The soldier's eyes settled on her face. 'Why should I tell you anything, *little girl*?'

Gwen drew her rapier, quick as lightning, and pressed the point into the exposed part of the soldier's neck. She leant close to him.

'Because this *little girl* is all that stands between you and death,' she hissed.

The soldier swallowed. 'All right,' he said, quickly. 'I work for General Gor, in the Hidden Mines.'

Castor snorted. 'Lies!' he said. 'The mines were abandoned long ago.'

Tanner saw Gwen press the sword-point harder into the fallen soldier's neck.

'I'm not lying,' he rushed out his words. 'We've been digging there since the winter at General Gor's orders. Opening up the old tunnels.'

'Digging for what?' asked Tanner.

The soldier shook his head and a trickle of blood escaped over his neck. He groaned in agony. 'Iron ore,' he said. 'The General wants a bigger army with more weapons. Captain Brutus has the slaves digging day and night. Others working an armoury underground. I haven't seen it with my own eyes, but you can hear the hammers and anvils at all hours.'

Gwen drew back her rapier. Tanner pulled his friend aside, and Castor followed.

'Have you been to the mines?' Tanner asked.

'Not inside, but I know where they are,' Castor replied.

'Could you show us exactly?' said Gwen. She had already taken out the map and laid it on the ground. Castor knelt beside her, frowning and tracing its surface with his finger.

'I've gone that way on Nera,' he muttered. 'It's up this valley,' he muttered. 'Over the pass and along to the third ridge.' He stabbed his finger at a spot located in the well between three peaks. 'Here!' he said.

Gwen looked at Tanner. 'That's where we'll find the mask,' she murmured.

'And now Geffen's told Derthsin exactly where to go – to the eastern tunnels,' said Tanner. 'Now that they've been opened up again, he'll have no problem getting there.'

'Who's Geffen?' asked Castor. 'What mask?'

Gwen sighed. 'Geffen's my brother,' she said. 'He was a brave fighter, though not as skilled as you.'

Tanner started to open his mouth to protest, but Gwen sent him a sly wink. He saw Castor grin with pride. *She's humouring him*, he realised. *Playing to Castor's ego.* He turned away to hide his smile.

She was a clever one, all right. 'He's betrayed us,' Gwen continued, 'and is leading our enemy to his prize.'

'The Mask of Death,' Tanner added, turning back. 'The pieces are scattered around Avantia. If Derthsin can gather them all, he'll have total power over the Beasts.'

Castor gave a low whistle and stood up. 'It sounds like you need a hero,' he said.

'And that would be you?' Gwen asked, folding her arms.

'Why not?' Castor grinned. 'There's nothing left in this town, and if it comes to a battle, you two will need someone to show you how to fight!'

Tanner and Gwen exchanged a glance. What were they taking on?

Castor jabbed his sword into the air, then clapped them both on the back.

'Thank you, Castor,' Gwen said, staggering forwards slightly.

Tanner nodded. 'It's good to have you with us.' Castor was a Chosen Rider – Tanner would just have to accept it. Their fates were intertwined.

The race is on!

Chapter Nine

'What are we waiting for?' said Castor.

Now that they were no longer fighting, Tanner could see that Castor's Beast had intricate markings on her fur. Her face was patterned with darker streaks, and patches of gold and chestnut rippled across her body. Nera batted at Castor playfully with her paw, claws gleaming as she pushed him up her side so that he was able to scramble onto her neck. He pressed his hand to the top of her head, and the Beast seemed to calm down.

'What will you do when you find your brother again?' he asked Gwen.

Gwen climbed onto Gulkien. The wolf shook himself and snapped at the air, as if he were stretching his jaws.

'I don't know,' she said quietly, staring straight ahead and refusing to look at either of them.

'We've all lost something or someone,' said

Tanner. 'But Derthsin's going to pay.'

As they were about to take off, Gwen cried, 'Wait! Castor, won't you be missed here? Isn't there anyone you need to say goodbye to?'

Tanner saw him tense.

'No. No one,' Castor said.

Gulkien and Firepos beat their wings and soared into the air, their shadows rippling over the village square. Firepos's feathers shone like bronze as they ruffled in the breeze, and Gulkien's fur flattened over his long snout. Nera raced ahead, across the land, leaping from hillock to valley, her tail flying out behind her. Tanner had never seen a Beast move so fast across land.

Castor and Nera led the way. From up above, the two other Beasts banked round until they were heading towards the Northern Mountains where the Hidden Mines were. Low, ugly grey clouds hung over the mountainside. Ahead of them, the ground was dark.

They passed through chilly clouds, towards

the steep, iron-grey faces of the Northern Mountains. The two winged Beasts flew single-file up a pass threaded with a silver stream, and the vegetation petered out below. Nera leapt from rock to rock, her claws sending out sparks. Nothing seemed to slow her down, not even the barren land and thin air.

Sharp-edged shadows were cast by the mountain rocks and jagged peaks. Boulders and crumbling drifts of black-slate rock wound like dry rivers up the mountains. Castor whistled, and Nera raced up a river bed, only to loop back – all in the time it had taken Gulkien and Firepos to fly the same distance. Castor called up: 'I bet your Beasts can't fly that fast!'

'Of course they can,' Tanner said, not wanting to admit the truth that Nera was faster.

Nera shot back and forth in maddening bursts. Firepos's feathers shook in the air with her steady wing beats, and Gulkien's wings creaked on the wind gusts. Nera was toying with them.

'Prove it,' Castor yelled. 'Let's see if you can keep up!'

'You're on!' Tanner called down. 'Oh, and Castor? If I beat you to the next mountain, you have to be quiet for the rest of the trip.'

Castor smiled and sat back, his hands behind his head, so he was only holding onto Nera with his thighs. 'And if I beat you,' Castor said, 'you have to give me your sword.'

'I'm not going to give you my sword, Castor.'

'Just until we get there,' Castor shouted. 'Besides, I thought you said your bird was fast.'

Tanner glanced at Gwen. 'All right, Castor. Ready…'

Castor said, 'Set…'

They hunched forward.

'Go!' Gwen yelled.

Tanner and Castor stared in astonishment as Gulkien streaked ahead of them, his paws tucked up underneath him, his leathery wings flapping hard.

'Now, Firepos!' Tanner shouted.

Castor yelled, 'Go, Nera!'

The boys and their Beasts raced after Gwen. Tanner held tightly onto Firepos's neck, his eyes streaming in the rushing air. She shot like an arrow after Gulkien, her wings close to her back.

Below Firepos, Nera ran in a rapid, frantic rhythm. Her huge paws thudded against the rocks and her coat rippled as she darted from boulder to mountain ledge.

Gulkien's movements in the air were more measured and even, whilst Firepos only used her wings occasionally, zooming as straight as a dagger through the sky. Tanner could hear Castor shouting encouragement to Nera below them.

As they burst over the pass at the end of the valley, Gulkien suddenly pulled back, directly into the path of Firepos. Nera jerked to a stop below them, and Firepos beat her wings to stay in the same spot of mountain air.

Castor shouted, 'What's the matter with you two? We're still racing!'

'No, we're not,' Gwen said.

'Why?' Castor demanded.

'Look.'

A black mountain range of three peaks loomed ahead of them. Plumes of grey-white smoke rose amid the summits. The mountains tapered into ugly spikes that seemed to stab at the sky, and as they flew closer, Tanner realised the smoke was coming from long slits in the high rock. *Vents*, he thought. *The kind an armoury would need.*

They flew between the peaks. Just as Castor had said, the inner slopes fell into a deep cavity, the bottom of which was filled with grey water. About halfway up the nearest black mountain, Tanner spotted a square entrance, braced with wooden supports like a mine shaft.

'Why aren't there guards outside?' Gwen called over the wind.

'Maybe Derthsin doesn't think he needs them,' Tanner said. 'Remember how his soldiers were attacking ordinary villagers, just because they could? Derthsin is overconfident.'

Castor urged Nera on. 'Beat you there!'

'Castor, wait!' Tanner shouted. The time for games was over. Firepos dived after them in a steep drop that made Tanner's stomach lurch. He gripped Firepos's feathers – the ground was rushing up too fast. Firepos pulled out of her dive, and glided to land at the cave entrance. Nera arrived beside her, and a moment later, Gulkien brought Gwen down. After they all dismounted from their Beasts, Gulkien began to stalk the area outside the cave, sniffing and growling. Firepos sat seriously, her head poised to watch the sky. Nera paced and scratched the rock impatiently, her gold fur rippling.

'Impressive,' Castor said. 'At least your bird knows how to dive.'

'That's enough!' Tanner snapped at him. He raised a finger to his lips. 'This place is dangerous. We need to be quiet.'

Tanner felt the ground trembling. Pebbles danced and shook, and as he approached the cave, he heard a heavy metallic clanking and banging. There was a distant hiss, like steam being released, and then the noise of metal striking metal sounded even louder.

A low voice boomed over the racket, barking unintelligible orders, bellowing from somewhere deep inside the earth. Tanner hesitated at the dark cave entrance. It sounded like the noise of dungeons and nightmares. He heard Castor and Gwen approach behind him.

'I'll see what's happening,' Tanner whispered. 'I'll go as far as I can without being seen.'

'We should all go,' Gwen said. 'Geffen might be in there.'

'No, it's too risky,' he said. 'Only one of us needs to see what's happening to come up with a plan.'

To Tanner's surprise, Castor didn't put up a fight. Instead, he stayed on Nera's back. His face was dark and unreadable. *His mood has changed*, Tanner thought.

'All right. We'll wait with the Beasts,' Gwen said.

'Be careful.'

Firepos squawked and shuffled closer. Tanner forced a smile. 'Don't worry. I'll be back before you know it.'

Secrets overheard

Chapter Ten

Tanner crept into the blackness. The passage went down, and, as it turned, the entrance disappeared around the corner behind him. Tanner paused to allow his eyes to adjust to the dark. Dim orange lanterns hung from hooks along the ceiling. The walls were lined with wooden support posts, and ahead the passage opened into a broad cavern. It felt like looking into the black heart of the earth.

The further Tanner crawled along, the more deafening the crash of metal became. The air stank of sulphur and acrid smoke stung Tanner's throat. Carefully, he slipped behind a rock wall. In the darkness, he fingered the scrap of linen tied around his wrist. Past a line of boulders, fires flickered and flashed, and beneath the voice shouting orders Tanner heard the sound of boys crying out.

'Faster! Move!' the booming voice yelled.

Tanner crouched low and crawled to a boulder

overlooking the armoury. It was hot, the air thick and hard to breathe. He peered around the side.

Below spread a cavern twice the size of the market square in Tanner's village. The ceiling was high, and lined with jagged stalactites. In the middle of the room an assembly of rusted, gaping furnaces had been installed back-to-back, with pipes that shot all the way up into the ceiling. Exhausted boys worked in lines, lugging overloaded wheelbarrows of rocks from carts at one end of the cave to the red-hot furnace fires.

Two sets of iron tracks ran into dark holes in the wall, presumably to the rock faces where the iron ore was being quarried. Boys worked the massive bellows, blasting air into the red-hot furnaces, while others poured liquid metal into stone casts. As they cooled, the strongest-looking boys hammered and sweated at long, iron-grey forges and anvils. Even these boys were so thin that Tanner could make out the bulge of their ribs through their burnt and ragged clothes. In the flickering light, Tanner saw that the rear wall was lined with wooden cages. Something writhed and glimmered from beneath the boys' feet. Eyes stared out between the bars.

Tanner's gaze was caught by the reflection of the furnace flames glinting on a heap of axe-heads and breastplates near the forges. A boy raised a conical helmet in the orange firelight.

They're being forced to make weapons that might be used to kill their own families, Tanner thought. His chest tightened with rage.

Guards in dark armour patrolled the work lines, armed with clubs. When a boy pushing a cart tripped and spilt a pile of black coal, one of the guards beat him until the boy crumpled, whimpering.

'Pick it up!' the guard yelled, raising his club over the cowering boy.

'Troublemaker?' said the deep voice Tanner had heard from outside the cave. A soldier stepped into view. He was a head taller than the rest of the guards, and his armour was covered with small, red-brown handprints and streaks. *Blood*, Tanner thought. The man carried a long, black whip.

'Captain Brutus,' the soldier said. 'This brat may be another candidate for the cages.'

'Is that true?' Captain Brutus said, his face twisted into a cruel grin. To the boy, he shouted, 'Get up, you lazy runt! You are here to work, not sleep. On your feet!'

The boy used the side of the coal-cart to pull himself up, but it tipped over, spilling coal. With a jerk, Brutus cracked his whip in front of the boy's face. Tanner felt himself flinch.

'No, please!' the boy begged.

Brutus turned to the nearby boys and guards watching the pitiful scene. 'Back to work! All of you. Or Troiden will be crunching on your bones before nightfall.'

Everyone returned to work. *Crack!* With an expert flick of his wrist, Brutus lashed out at a boy who hadn't moved fast enough, and then the captain raised his whip at the nearest guard. 'You put this brat in the cages! There should be a fresh supply of snakes in there, by now.' He brought his face close to the sobbing boy and imitated a snake's hiss. 'They'll like meeting you.' With that, Brutus strode away.

Tanner was breathing hard, his hands balled into fists. He dripped with sweat as he eased himself back, away from the boulder. Pressed against the wall, and gripping his sword tight, he crept into the recesses of the caverns.

He reached a fork. Blazing light cast flickering shadows down one tunnel, the other was black as a starless night. Steeling himself, he took the dark passage. He had a sense of Firepos sending him encouragement. *Keep going. Stay strong.*

Feeling his way with just the fingertips of one hand, Tanner noticed the air cool. *I must be heading away from the furnaces and into the mine.* Who or what was Troiden? What lived down here in the darkness of the Hidden Mines?

Gradually, his ears picked out the ringing of pickaxes on rock. This must have been another route to the rock faces, deep in the mountain. He made out stairs, cut into the tunnel, and heard water dripping in the gloom. Tanner took a few more steps around a gentle bend, and paused. Dim torchlight cast red shadows on the wall opposite a roughly hewn, arched door.

'…they will find it soon,' said a gravelly voice. A voice he had heard before.

Tanner edged closer, feeling his heart knocking in his chest.

'Our enemies draw near,' said another voice, like a whisper of dead leaves. 'I *feel* them.'

'They're only children,' scoffed General Gor impatiently.

Tanner reached the doorway and looked through. Within was a simple chamber. Gor, dressed in his black armour, stood with his back to Tanner, and beside him was Captain Brutus.

There was a third person – a man in a cloak.

Tanner knew that if the man turned he would see a scar snaking across his face and throat. It was Vendrake. The three of them were addressing a low flame that flickered yellow and green. There was the figure he'd seen before amidst flames: Derthsin. Even from this distance, Tanner could see the ugly scars on his face and the glow of evil in his eyes. *Where is he?* Tanner wondered. *Why does he need to send visions of himself? Where is he hiding?*

'They may only be children,' hissed Derthsin, 'but they control powerful allies. And now I fear they may have found a third.'

It took Tanner a moment to realise that Derthsin was talking about him and his friends. *Children?* Gor turned and the firelight captured his cruel profile.

'We have the boy back, at least,' said Gor. 'Vendrake forced the truth from him. He has told us where to look.'

'We're opening up the eastern tunnels,'

added Captain Brutus. 'If we concentrate our manpower there, it cannot be long until we have what you seek.'

The piece of the mask! Tanner thought.

'And what shall we do with the boy then?' asked Vendrake.

The image of Derthsin seemed to glow brighter than before. 'He is of no more use to us. We won't need to arrange any further meetings with him. Feed him to the Troiden.'

Tanner backed away from the doorway. Picking his way carefully, he hurried along the passage towards the light. He emerged, coughing on the filthy air, then hurried outside. Gwen and Castor were waiting, peering from behind a rocky outcrop, their eyes wide. The Beasts were perched on the mountain above them.

'So?' Castor demanded.

Tanner filled his lungs with clean, mountain air. 'They're making weapons,' he reported. 'And armour too. The boys are slaves – they're working the furnaces and forges. It's horrible.'

'And Geffen?' Gwen asked quickly.

Tanner hesitated. 'He's told them to look for the mask in the eastern tunnels, but…' He wasn't sure he could find the words.

'Say it,' Gwen hissed. 'Whatever it is, just say it.'

'As soon as they find the piece of the mask, they're going to kill him. I was right – he'd arranged to meet Gor when he sneaked away from our camp. But now, he's no more use to them.' His words came out in a rush. He told them what he'd seen, about Captain Brutus, Vendrake and Gor, and the image of Derthsin in the flames. About Troiden.

'What about the boys?' Castor said.

Tanner's voice cracked. 'They're starving. They're being beaten and overworked and… some of them are in cages with snakes.'

'*Snakes?*' Gwen repeated.

'Trapped like animals,' Castor said. He

paced in a slow circle. 'The boys I grew up with…
I should be with them…' He punched the rock,
shaking with rage. He hit the rock until his
knuckles were streaked with blood.

*My feathers ruffle with a prickle of emotion. Castor is full
of secrets and pain. One glance into Nera's face tells me
that. Does Tanner know what secrets lie in his new friend's
heart? I think he suspects.*

*I close my eyes and listen to whatever the boy's soul is
flooded with. Ah, yes… Guilt.*

*I understand. My eyes snap open. Self-loathing infects
the boy, like a disease. The tremor in his eyes, the shake of
his hands – what is he hiding?*

'Castor!' Tanner grabbed him. 'Calm down.'

'Those are my people,' Castor shouted. 'Let go!'
He shook Tanner away and drew his sword. Tanner
noticed for the first time that it had the emblem
of a cat's claw embedded in the hilt. 'We're going
to free them now. I'll go first…' Castor said.

Tanner grabbed him by the shoulders, yanking him away from the cave entrance.

'Listen to me,' he said, keeping his voice as steady as he could. 'We'll save them, I promise. But we can't do it like this. Even if we could beat the guards – and there are *a lot* of soldiers – if we charge in like this, they may hurt more of the boys before we can stop them. And we may not even get near the piece of the Mask of Death. We have to think of a plan.'

Castor was shaking his head, but he was beginning to calm down. 'What, then?'

Tanner thought for a moment. 'I don't just want to save the boys and find the mask. I want to destroy the armoury, so those weapons are never used to bring more harm to Avantia. To do that, we need to get close to their leader, Captain Brutus, and his men. Overpower them. So we need to get in without being noticed.'

'Great,' Castor said. 'But *how*?'

'There must be a way, I don't know…'

'Disguises,' Gwen said. Tanner turned to her. 'We'll disguise ourselves as captured boys from Castor's town. We'll blend in and slip past the soldiers. Then we can get close enough to free the boys and find a way to destroy the armoury.'

Castor sighed. 'You make it sound so easy.'

'It's a good plan,' Tanner said, clapping Gwen on the shoulder. 'We *will* make them pay for what they've done.'

Castor nodded and put his sword away.

'It's down to us,' Tanner said.

Nera roars, the mountain shakes

Chapter Eleven

Tanner tugged on a sleeve of his tunic until it ripped and unravelled. He grabbed a handful of dirt and smeared it in brown streaks across his clothes. Castor and Gwen did the same. All three of them tore at their tunics, making them ragged and loose. They crushed sandy rock into their hair and patted it across their faces and skin. When they were finished, their faces were so filthy that their eyes seemed startlingly bright.

'How's that?' Tanner said.

Castor studied him, then raised a fistful of dirt. 'You need more on your chin.' He slapped a black streak across Tanner's face.

Tanner laughed and coughed. 'I'm pretty sure you could use some more too,' he said.

Castor jumped back, grinning, and Tanner threw a dirt clod at him.

'What about me?' Gwen said. 'How do I look?'

Tanner examined her. Gwen's tunic was

crumpled and jagged at the ends, and her trousers were so dirty that she trailed dust when she moved.

'Looks good to me,' Castor said.

'Except for one thing,' Tanner said. 'Your hair.'

Gwen raised a hand to her long, tangled plaits. They were caked in debris and dirt, but they were still too long. If the guards saw her blonde hair, they'd realise straightaway that she didn't belong.

'What do we do?' Gwen asked.

'Simple,' Castor said, and he stepped close to grab a lock of her hair. He started to draw his sword.

'No!' Gwen backed away. 'You are *not* cutting it off.'

'It's too long,' Castor said. 'You don't look anything like a boy.'

'He's right,' Tanner agreed.

Gwen yanked up the collar of her tunic and tucked her long hair down the back. 'There – it's dark in the cave, isn't it? No one will notice.'

Castor shook his head. 'This is foolish. If they see we've got a *girl* with us…'

'I'm coming with you.' Gwen's voice was steady and fierce. She stared him down. 'They attacked my village. They have my brother. This is my battle, too.'

Before Castor could argue, Tanner said, 'Gwen will fight alongside us. She battles harder than any *boy* I've met.'

Castor shrugged.

The Beasts watched as Tanner, Castor, and Gwen approached the cave entrance, and when she saw Castor step towards the passageway, Nera bounded to block the opening. Towering between Castor and the cave, Nera clawed the ground, her golden fur standing on end as her claws sent out a spray of sparks.

'We'll be careful,' Castor told her.

But Nera didn't move, and when he tried to step past her, she reared back and roared. The sudden, deafening noise jolted Tanner backwards.

He dodged as a shower of mountain rocks cascaded down around them, shattering to pieces when they hit the ground. At the edge of the cave entrance, a small rockslide tumbled down, breaking free of the mountain. The rockslide came to a halt and the air filled with dust from the debris.

'That's it!' Tanner cried. 'Castor, can Nera cause the caves to collapse? Could she bury the entire armoury?'

Castor nodded. 'I think so.' He climbed onto Nera's back and leant close to her face. 'Nera, go to the top of the mountain,' he said. 'Can you give us time to save the boys?' He waited, anxious as Nera glanced at the other Beasts, then at Tanner and Gwen. 'Please, Nera,' Castor said. 'At the top of the mountain, your roar can break the stone. You can bring it all down.' Nera retracted her claws, a fierce intelligence burning in her eyes. 'For me,' Castor said, climbing back to the ground. She lowered her head so that he could run his hand behind her ears. 'Be careful,' he said, and Nera leapt onto the rock, her fur rippling gold as she climbed.

Nera clambered up the mountainside, her claws hooking and scraping the stone. The Beast cast a long shadow as she arched overhead. Tanner watched her race above them, getting smaller as she ran towards the summit of the black mountain. Firepos sat straight, watching the mountain peak, while Gulkien sniffed and clicked his fangs, growling low.

'Do you think Nera can really cause the caves to crumble?' Gwen said.

'You saw what she did,' Castor said proudly. 'And she wasn't even trying. If she goes to the top and doesn't hold back…' He grinned. 'She'll bring down the mountain.'

'Burying the armoury,' Tanner added. 'I think it's our best chance. Come on.'

Hoping they were doing the right thing, he led the way back underground.

*

We watch the Chosen Riders disappear into the open jaw of darkness in the side of the mountain. My heart goes with them; we can do nothing to protect them now. But I am certain that fate has brought us here, and I know that Nera will do all she can to help. There is no turning back. I glance up at my fellow Beast and, even from this distance, see her fur rippling with anticipation. Low clouds are rolling in, shutting out the daylight.

The emptiness of death draws near. Gulkien snorts at the air, as if he can smell it. Something terrible is coming – a fight to the death. I can only wait and watch the darkness grow around me. In the dimming light, the world becomes smaller, suffocating. Time passes. Let fate spare the Chosen Riders; let them know what to do.

Derthin's mine

Chapter Twelve

Tanner and his companions followed the orange lanterns along the cave passage, their shadows flickering and dancing on the dark walls. The clang and clatter of the armoury grew louder, the air more sour with smoke. Tanner signalled to Castor and Gwen to stop when they reached the broad opening of the cavern. He saw the anger on both of their faces as they heard the boys screaming and men shouting.

'We need to keep low to the ground,' Tanner hissed. They dropped to their stomachs and crawled to the first boulder. When they were close enough to see the armoury, Gwen gasped.

'They're so thin,' she murmured.

Castor's fists were clenched, his jaw set.

Below, the boys were still working, the guards pacing among them with clubs. One led a prowling varkule on a chain. It snapped its jaws left and right, bringing panicked wails from the workers.

Captain Brutus cracked his whip past the head of a dark-haired boy who was pouring molten metal into a mould. The boy flinched as the whip just missed his face.

'Faster!' Brutus shouted. 'Finish that axe-head before I come back or I'll cut off one of your ears. Do you hear me?'

'Y-yes,' the boy said.

Captain Brutus stalked away and pointed at a boy working the furnaces. Each time furnace sparks flared, Brutus's armour glittered a bloody crimson. 'Move that ore. Faster!'

The captain's back was turned – this was their chance. Tanner carefully crept around the rocks, slowly…

'Now!' Castor said, and he darted down, towards a line of boys hammering at the forge. There was a guard in between Castor and the boys.

'Castor!' Tanner hissed. What was the fool doing?

But it was too late to stop him. Tanner grabbed

Gwen's hand and they ran down too. Staying low to the ground, they rushed across the open cavern, then stopped as the guard started to turn towards them – Castor froze in plain view.

'Look out!' Tanner hissed. He and Gwen ran directly towards Castor and the guard. The boys saw what was happening. Tanner swiped his hand at them: *stay quiet*. He grabbed Castor's arm and hustled Gwen and Castor in a quick sidestep around the guard's back to the forge. The boys stared as Tanner, Castor and Gwen slipped beside them.

'Now what?' Gwen panted.

Tanner drew his own sword and placed it on the anvil, then grabbed a hammer from a nearby rack. 'Pretend to work.'

Gwen found another hammer and they took it in turns to bring them down on the anvil. Castor picked up a shovel and began to hurl coal into the furnace grate.

'The guards will see,' one of the captive boys

whispered to his neighbour. 'We're going to get in trouble for this…'

Another boy murmured, 'What should we do?'

Tanner swung his hammer high and brought it down on the anvil. In between blows he looked around him, trying to spot a pattern to the guards' and Captain Brutus's movements. *We don't have much time*, he thought. *We need to make our move before the guards spot us.* He counted two guards by the rear cages and another seven watching the work lines. They were all armed with clubs and dressed in armour. But the captive boys outnumbered the guards at least five to one, and maybe ten to one if he included those in the cages.

Gwen was watching Captain Brutus, not paying attention as she pretended to hammer. She bent her head and a coil of golden hair snaked out at her nape, falling down her back.

'Gwen, your hair!' Castor hissed.

She froze, dropped her hammer and stuffed her plaits back down her tunic. The guards were still patrolling, oblivious, but the boys working around them had noticed. They turned to the dark-haired boy Captain Brutus had threatened, as if he were in charge.

'Should we tell the guards?' one boy asked him. 'Brutus will whip us if we don't.'

The dark-haired boy shook his head, and moved beside Tanner. 'Who are you?' he asked. His voice shook, but Tanner saw hope in his eyes. 'Are you here to rescue us?'

Before Tanner could say anything, the other boys stopped work and crowded around him.

'You are!' another boy gasped. 'Why else would you be here?'

The boys' voices rose as the news passed through their ranks, and Captain Brutus looked round. He came striding over, his armour creaking. Tanner kept his eyes on his anvil, not daring to look up.

'No talking or I'll nail your tongues to the wall!' the captain bellowed.

They turned back to their work, hammering without speaking until Brutus strode away.

'Yes,' Tanner said quietly, watching Brutus's massive, retreating back. 'We're going to get you all out of here. But don't stop working!'

Captain Brutus looked over at them again, but the boys were all hammering in silence.

'I'm Corrin,' the dark-haired boy whispered.

'Corrin?' Gwen exclaimed. 'From Colton? Your grandmother told us about you!'

Sudden tears sprang up in Corrin's eyes, spilling over his cheeks, and leaving trails through the soot that stained his cheeks. He wiped them away with a ragged sleeve. 'My grandmother is alive! She survived!'

Gwen nodded, pressing his hand with her own.

'Shh!' Castor said sharply. 'Be quiet.' He turned to Tanner. 'So, what's the plan?'

Tanner motioned to Gwen, Castor and Corrin to lean in. 'Castor, you and I will take on Captain

Brutus next time he comes past. Gwen, you open the cages.' Tanner looked at Corrin. 'You and the other boys need to attack the guards so Gwen can free the boys from the cages.'

Corrin nodded eagerly. 'I understand. But what about the others who've been taken to the eastern tunnels?'

'I'll handle that,' said Tanner. *Though I'm not quite sure how.*

Captain Brutus was taunting the boys in the cages, flicking his whip between the bars. He turned and started to make his way back towards the forges.

Tanner felt his heart racing. *If this doesn't work*, he thought, *we're all going to meet our deaths in these tunnels.*

Aloud, he murmured, 'Arm the boys, Corrin.'

Corrin nodded and passed finished swords down the line of boys.

'*Now*,' Castor said, his neck and face tense.

'Not yet,' Tanner hissed sharply.

Captain Brutus came closer. He was at the next furnace…

'You,' Captain Brutus said, pointing his whip at Corrin. 'Have you finished making that axe-head yet? Or do you owe me an ear?'

Tanner saw Gwen tense. Castor was holding the coal shovel with both hands, ready to swing it. They all kept their faces down and Tanner slid his hand towards the hilt of his sword. Captain Brutus was only a few paces away.

Almost, Tanner thought. His grip tightened on his sword.

'Hey, boy!' Captain Brutus shouted at Tanner. 'Hammer that blade, you stupid little maggot!' Then he stopped in his tracks. 'Where did you get that sword?' he snarled. 'That blade isn't from this armoury!'

Tanner gave a tiny nod to Gwen and Castor, and raised the sword. 'Go!'

Blade versus whip

Chapter Thirteen

Tanner vaulted the forge towards Captain Brutus, and Castor charged from the right with the shovel.

Brutus raised the whip over his shoulder. 'You little fools!'

He whirled towards Castor, who tried to dodge. Tanner winced as the whip sliced over Castor's head. He leapt forward, stabbing at the captain, but the big man turned aside, and his sword only gouged across his breastplate.

Brutus thumped him with a meaty fist, sending Tanner stumbling towards his friend. Castor threw the shovel aside and drew his sword, but the Captain laughed, an ugly noise that thundered round the cavern.

'Drop your weapons, and I'll only cut off one of your hands. I'll even let you choose which one.'

He paced towards Castor and Tanner, flicking

his whip and forcing them away from the forge, towards a rock wall. 'I'll take your fingers off, boys. I'll dip them in your own blood…' – he tapped his armour – '…and add them to my collection.'

As Brutus forced him back, Tanner could see that Gwen had slipped away from the forge towards the cages. She was gesturing desperately to Corrin, but he and the other boys were all frozen to the spot, watching the fight through wide, frightened eyes. Two guards must have spotted the swords in their hands, because they walked over with their clubs. Another came from a different part of the cavern, leading a varkule. The animal's ears were erect and the striped fur on his spine stood up as he snarled, sending out a putrid smell.

The plan's not working, Tanner thought, panic bubbling through him. *If the boys don't fight, there's no way we can get out of here…*

Brutus's whip snaked through the air again. It caught the heel of Castor's boot and pulled him off-balance. He landed with a thud, his sword clattering to the ground. Brutus snapped the whip and it cracked against the stone floor in a spray of tiny rocks, a hair's breadth from Castor's face.

Tanner raised his sword, ready to attack, but Brutus was surprisingly quick. He lashed out, and Tanner felt the cut of the whip around his wrist. Brutus grinned as he pulled Tanner towards him. With his other hand he seized a hammer from beside the anvil. 'I'll bash your brains out, boy!'

Tanner could do nothing as he was dragged across the floor. His sword arm, held tight, was useless. Brutus raised the hammer. On the ground at the captain's feet, Tanner saw Castor shaking his head free of dizziness. Castor reached into his belt for his dagger. With a lunge, he buried the tip in Brutus's foot.

The captain bellowed in pain and dropped his whip, falling backwards to clutch at the dagger. Tanner untangled his hand from the leather. His arm was soaked with blood.

'Now!' Gwen yelled.

Tanner saw her draw a pair of throwing axes from her tunic and charge the nearest guard. She chopped into his club with one axe and swung her other axe at his head – he dodged, but she yanked away his club, which was still embedded in her axe. 'Help me,' she called to Corrin. 'We're here to get you out, but you have to fight – all of you!'

Corrin and the other boys raised the weapons they had been working on. They ran to attack, crying out angrily, their chests heaving as blades were brought down on the guards. In the chaos, Tanner saw the varkule rear as the boys swarmed over it, stabbing and hacking. Lips curled back from his yellow teeth as the boys punched and stabbed; soon the varkule lay in the dirt with blood pooling around his fur. The boys swarmed over the body, raising their blades against soldiers who backed away, their eyes wide.

'Hurry!' Tanner shouted, as Gwen hacked at the thick cage bars. 'We need to get to the eastern tunnels before it's too late.'

The cage splintered but it didn't break.

Castor was cornered, blood trickling down his shoulder, his sword gripped with both hands. Captain Brutus limped towards him. 'I haven't finished with you yet.'

'Hey!' Tanner called. 'Brutus!'

Captain Brutus spun towards him. Tanner feinted left, and when Brutus swung his whip, Tanner leapt right, onto a coal-cart. The cart capsized behind him as Tanner jumped off, bringing his feet forward and slamming his boots into the centre of Brutus's chest. The impact knocked Tanner down, but it also rattled Brutus's breastplate loose. The captain tripped and fell backwards with a cry.

Castor brought his blade round and sliced Brutus's whip in half. It fell to the ground.

There was a splintering sound of wood cracking.

Gwen had broken open the first cage. Snakes slithered across the cave floor towards dark corners. A boy scrambled out, and despite his starved, emaciated limbs, he grabbed a hammer from a nearby rack and charged at an injured guard crawling across the ground with his sword.

'Get back!' ordered the guard, but the boy batted the guard's sword clean out of his grasp. Without hesitation, the boy brought the hammer back up and smashed it into the guard's face. Blood spurted from his nostrils as he fell backwards. Other boys drove their blades into his side in fast, deadly stabs. He collapsed face down, and lay motionless.

But more guards streamed into the cavern, carrying swords and shields. Tanner knew they must have been alerted by the sounds.

Corrin led the boys in a war cry as they grabbed rocks, swords, hammers and clubs, to help Gwen break open the remaining cages and free the boys trapped inside.

Captain Brutus climbed to his feet. His breastplate slipped off and crashed to the floor, exposing a black tunic. Gesturing with his ruined whip, he yelled at the incoming guards. 'Kill them! Get into your formations. They're only children – cut them down.'

'Gwen!' Tanner yelled. 'Rally the boys. Don't let them give up.'

Gwen gave him a sharp nod, and directed Corrin and some of the older boys towards the new attackers. She'd lost one of her axes, but raised another defiantly, and drew her rapier with her free hand. She shouted across at Tanner, 'We can't hold them for long!'

Tanner just had time to duck as something flew past his head and clattered into the forge behind him. Brutus was using his massive strength to hurl shields from a heap of armour at them. In between throws, he ordered the guards to fight their way across the cavern and to form groups, back-to-back. The guards rushed the boys, knocking them back in a clatter of swords. They cried out in pain and fell as the guards trampled them to the ground. The tide was turning again.

'You can't win,' Brutus sneered at Tanner and Castor.

'Oh, I think we can,' Castor said, and he nodded to Tanner. 'Where's Firepos?'

Of course! Tanner thought. The tunnel was small, but the Beasts might be able to squeeze through – it was worth a try.

'Firepos!' he shouted.

Gwen heard him and joined the cry. 'Gulkien!'

I hear something…a cry from deep in the mountain. Gulkien springs towards the cave entrance. When he looks back at me, I see the anger in his eyes. The Chosen Riders are in danger. They are calling for help.

Tucking my feathers against my flanks, I follow Gulkien into the darkness. My talons grip rock, pulling me through the tunnel. My feathers brush and tear against the walls. Ahead, the sound of clashing metal and blood-cries echo. The tunnel widens. I spread my wings, and screech into the cavern, fire blazing across my wings.

With a ferocious roar, Gulkien leaps onto an armed man, his fangs and gums bared, his yellow eyes flashing. The shouts of triumph turn to screams of terror.

I swoop over the evil men that have surrounded the Chosen Riders. There are smaller boys too, who must be protected. Their faces brighten with terror and awe as I open my wings and call out my war cry. The evil men scatter around me, wailing for help.

As the men form groups, I dart between stalactites, then drop low to hook my beak into a man's shoulder. He screams as I fly higher with him. The men shout and point, their faces lit with terror, and I toss my catch across the cavern. He hits the wall hard and lands in a crumpled heap of broken limbs.

A man raises his shield at me – I catch it in my claws, bending the metal back on itself. Fire flares from my talons, engulfing him like a human torch.

He moans in the crackle of flames.

Below, Gulkien lunges at another man, who drops his sword to cower behind an anvil. Growling, Gulkien backs a trio of men towards the far cavern wall. They wave spears at him, but he swats them aside with his massive paws and shakes the life from his foes.

'Help!' the girl calls to us. 'The cages!'

Evil men have formed a wall of shields and blades to guard their captured boys. The children are locked behind wooden bars. I understand; I can tell Gulkien does too.

I can see the horror in the men, the way their swords shiver. My friend, the wolf-Beast, stalks towards them. When he snarls, his eyes wide in the firelight, the line of men staggers back. I fly behind the furnace, and, as Gulkien leaps closer, the men turn — directly into me. I crash into their shields, shrieking as they fall over each other, struggling to get out of my way. I snap my beak, and Gulkien smashes them to the ground.

I am Firepos. Fear me.

Brutus laughed, a low, ragged sound, and casually walked to a weapon rack. He seemed to have no fear of either Beast and fixed his eyes on Tanner and Castor as he grabbed a heavy club that was shaped like a sharp, grinning skull, with long black spikes on the end. The spikes gleamed in the orange light cast from torches ranged along the cave walls.

Brutus pointed the weapon at Castor, then at Tanner. 'Now, who wants to die first?'

Tanner charged, swinging for Brutus's throat, and when Brutus blocked his blade, Castor came in fast, stabbing and swiping in quick thrusts that made Brutus stagger backwards. His club was short, but he moved it in efficient, defensive circles, expertly knocking their swords away. When the club connected with Tanner's blade, his whole arm shook with the impact.

'Peasants!' he spat. 'You don't deserve to live.'

But Tanner could see the panic in his face. They were pushing Brutus back. He couldn't attack, only defend himself from their blows. *We need to get closer*, Tanner thought.

Brutus forced Castor's sword down again, twisted back, and stopped Tanner's sword near his chest. He shoved Tanner away and blocked Castor again. They had nearly forced Brutus right against the wall – and Tanner saw his chance.

'Castor, brace yourself!'

Immediately understanding, Castor put his hands to his knees to create a springboard. Tanner ran and jumped, planting his feet on Castor's back and launching himself at Brutus. Brutus swung his club and missed – and Tanner kicked his heel into the man's chin, sending his head jerking back. Tanner landed in the dirt behind him.

'You filthy little runt!' Blood ran down Brutus's face. Tanner came up behind him and wrapped an arm around his throat, bringing his sword down and twisting it behind Brutus's club, hooking it the same way Castor had trapped the skinny boy's sword back in Colton. Tanner yanked up, but Brutus was too strong. The captain's free arm locked on the back of Tanner's neck, his fingers grasping his throat. Both of Brutus's arms were up in the air – his left gripping the locked club, his right on Tanner's throat.

'Now!' Tanner choked out.

With a roar, Castor drove his sword through Brutus's chest.

The captain made a startled, wet noise. His fingers fell limply from Tanner's neck and he dropped his club. As Castor pulled out his sword, the captain crumpled to his knees. Tanner jumped free and watched Brutus slump. He choked out a clot of blood. 'You…' His lips moved, but no further sound emerged.

Castor stepped back from the body. He stretched his wounded shoulder and wiped the blood from his sword. 'That's for the men of Colton,' he said.

Fighting for breath, Tanner stared at Brutus's sagging corpse. The blood pooling around the captain's gaping mouth was already darkening.

Gulkien and Firepos were corralling the last

of the soldiers, who realised that fighting on was useless. They dropped their swords. Gwen and Corrin gathered the boys around the forge. All of them carried weapons, and most were smeared with the blood of their captors.

'We did it!' Castor shouted.

Gwen looked at Tanner, her face tense. She was thinking the same thing.

It's not over yet.

Geffen's pleas go unanswered

Chapter Fourteen

'Castor,' said Tanner. 'Get the boys out with Gwen, before more guards come.'

'Where are you going?' he asked.

'I have to get to the next piece of the mask,' said Tanner. They'd already lost one, thanks to Geffen – he wasn't going to allow another to slip through his hands. He turned to Corrin. 'Which way to the eastern tunnels?'

The terrified boy shook his head. 'You can't. That's where the Troiden lives.'

A murmur passed through the boys.

'That's where I have to go,' said Tanner.

Corrin pointed a shaky finger at one of the carts on the tracks. 'That one,' he said.

'I'll come with you,' said Castor.

'You need to go to Nera,' Tanner said. 'You're the only one who can make her bring down the cavern.'

He climbed into the cart. It was fastened with

rope to a pulley. He lifted his sword, but Gwen caught his arm. 'You don't know what's down there!'

'I do,' he said. 'That's why I have to go. We can't risk Derthsin finding the next piece of the mask.'

Gwen's face softened, but she quickly clambered in beside Tanner. 'There's something precious to me down there, too. My brother.'

Tanner thought about arguing, but there wasn't time. He looked at Castor. 'If you hear more guards coming, you know what to do. Give Nera the word.'

'But you'll be inside!' said Castor.

'So will all the evil in Avantia,' said Tanner. 'Promise me you'll do it.'

Castor nodded, his face streaked with dirt and blood. 'Good luck.'

Tanner brought his sword down on the pulley rope, slicing through. The cart's wheels began to turn, and they trundled into the tunnel.

The fire-glow of the forges was lost as they plunged into blackness, picking up speed. The *rat-a-tat* of the cart's wheels grew faster and faster and the air rushed overhead. Tanner leant over the edge, and saw the dim tunnel walls flash past. They were going deep into the mountain, where their Beast protectors couldn't follow.

'What's the Troiden?' asked Gwen.

'I heard Derthsin mention it,' said Tanner, thinking back to the fear in the children's faces. 'I think it's a Beast of some sort.'

Gwen didn't say more.

Sparks arced off the wheels as the cart screeched around a corner. Then the track seemed to level off.

'We're slowing down,' said Tanner.

He peered out over the rim, and saw that the tunnel had widened and there was a weak light ahead. Then he saw shapes looming up on the track. More carts, stationary ones, and they were heading straight towards them.

'Look out!' he said, ducking back inside just as their cart clanged into another and they were thrown hard against the front.

'Nice landing,' whispered Gwen.

Tanner smiled grimly. 'We must be here.'

He was about to stand, when a voice nearby said, 'What was that noise?'

'Looks like a loose cart,' said another, closer still. 'Brutus must not be watching 'em properly up there.'

'Just a moment.' Tanner heard footsteps approaching and glimpsed the glow of a torch. He put a finger to his lips and drew his sword quietly. Gwen clutched her wolf-hilt rapier. A shadow fell across the cart. There was a half-grunt of surprise before Tanner smashed his hilt down on the man's temple. He flopped against the cart, and the torch fell to the ground.

'Breen?' said the other voice. 'What's wrong?'

'Come on,' Gwen hissed.

Tanner snatched up the torch, and they crept past the row of empty, waiting carts. Tanner strained his eyes and ears. The clanging of pickaxes he'd heard before seemed to have died, and he wondered if Corrin had been wrong. Perhaps these weren't the mines after all. Finally they reached a loading area, which seemed to have been abandoned. Shovels and half-filled carts stood idle.

'Where are all the miners?' said Gwen.

Tanner was looking at the tunnel walls. Great gouges seemed to have been taken out of the rock, far too wide for any pickaxe to have made them. White gashes had been clawed out of the sides of the tunnel. They seemed almost…natural.

More tunnels branched off from the one they were in, all leading into blackness.

'Which way *now*?' said Gwen.

'We should take a closer look,' Tanner replied. He took a few steps into one of the branches, but saw and heard nothing ahead. He went into the next. Gwen did the same in those on the other side of the main tunnel.

Tanner was beginning to lose hope, when she called to him.

'This way!'

Tanner darted across the tunnel to where she was standing, head cocked.

'I hear something,' she said.

Tanner listened too. She was right. Ahead was a sound like a distant grinding of machinery. Tanner found his steps quickening to a run, the fire from the torch flickering.

The sounds grew louder, and he saw more light in front of them. He tossed the torch aside. They wouldn't need it now.

Suddenly there was movement ahead.

'But I did what you asked!' shouted a voice.

Gwen let out a small whimper of fear. *Geffen.*

General Gor dragged Geffen by the scruff of his collar around the corner and away from them. Four guards followed in his wake, with

Vendrake bringing up the rear.

'The thing about traitors is that they can't be trusted,' said Gor. 'You have outlived your usefulness.'

'But he promised! I told you more than the map could! I, I…' His face flushed red. 'I have other secrets!' he said desperately.

Gor shook his head in disgust. 'You'd spill all your secrets, just like that? What a coward you are. You don't deserve to live.'

Beside Tanner, Gwen bolted out before he could pull her back.

'Let my brother go!' she said.

All the figures spun around, and the guards drew their swords. Tanner emerged beside Gwen.

'How did you get in here?' snapped Gor, his black eyes flashing. 'Where's Brutus?'

'The captain's dead,' said Tanner. 'Soon the armoury will be destroyed under half a mountain, and you will be buried with it.'

Gor barked a harsh laugh. 'Brutus was a fool.

You really think Derthsin cares about the armoury?' he said. 'He'll soon have what he wants, and an army more powerful than any you can imagine.'

The general pulled his cloak aside, and at his waist hung something Tanner had seen only in broken dreams: the next torn piece of the mask. This section was a cheekbone and part of the nose guard extending down the jaw. Beside it dangled the piece of the mask that Tanner had rescued, only for Geffen to steal it. Clearly, Gwen's twin had handed it over to the general.

'Your pathetic grandmother and her minion, Jonas, did well to hide the piece here,' said Gor.

Jonas! So he knew about the mapmaker.

'But my master will not be stopped. He grows stronger all the time.'

Tanner's anger fired his blood, and it burned through his veins.

'There are still two pieces to find,' Gwen said. 'And we have the map. We're strong, too.'

'Keep your map,' said Gor, closing his cloak. 'Your snivelling brother has told us where to look. You have nothing to look forward to but your death.' He pointed to the guard nearest Geffen. 'Bring the traitor to the Troiden. He'll appreciate a meal other than rock. The rest of you, kill these two.'

Gor turned and strode away down the tunnel. Geffen wailed as a soldier plucked him off the floor and followed. Geffen threw a last, desperate glance in his sister's direction but Gwen stood fixed to the spot, her eyes wide as she watched her brother being dragged away. The remaining three soldiers closed in on Tanner and Gwen, their blades glittering wickedly in the torch-lit tunnel.

The Troiden feeds

Chapter Fifteen

Tanner and Gwen backed away, their weapons held out in front of them.

'Three of us against two,' sneered one of the soldiers. 'This will be fun.'

Tanner found himself back where he'd dropped the torch. It was still lit, spitting embers on the ground. The faces of the guards were cast in deep shadows.

With every wasted moment, Gor was escaping with two pieces of the mask, and Geffen's peril grew.

Tanner stepped backwards over the fallen torch and turned to Gwen. 'Ready?' he whispered.

'Always.'

Tanner flicked the torch up with his toe, and it spun through the air at one of the guards. With a cry of surprise, he dodged sideways, clattering into his neighbour.

'You fool!' the guard said.

Tanner lunged, slicing his blade downwards across the guard's face, opening up a long cut. Screaming, the injured guard clutched his face and stumbled backwards. Gwen went down on one knee beneath an overhead blow, pulled out an axe from her belt, and buried the blade in the soldier's thigh.

'The odds look better now, don't they?' said Tanner.

The last soldier looked at his own sword unsurely.

'If I let you go…' he started to offer.

'Don't you mean if *we* let *you* go?' Tanner asked. He could hardly believe how calm his own voice sounded. *I'm learning how to do this.*

The man looked from Tanner to Gwen. She flicked back her cloak and he spotted two other axes lined up in her belt, waiting to be used.

'I, I…' the man stuttered. He looked at Tanner, his eyes pleading. Then he turned and ran into the darkness.

'After him!' yelled Gwen.

Tanner and his friend sprinted along the tunnel, but the man had a head start and was soon out of sight. Tanner glanced around. *This is the way Gor left.* They caught up with other fleeing soldiers, who cast fearful glances back. Tanner heard the pounding of hooves, and General Gor crashed into the guards on his stallion. A man crumpled beneath the horse's hooves; the sound of his ribs cracking reverberated off the tunnel walls.

Gor rode on without breaking stride. Riding Varlot. There was a flicker of intelligence in the stallion's eyes as he passed, but no sign of him morphing into his Beast self.

Tanner and Gwen watched Gor galloping away. The two pieces of the mask bounced by his side, dangling from his leather belt. Tanner knew it was pointless to go after him; he couldn't outrun such a powerful Beast.

'We have to find Geffen,' he said, pointing the way Gor had come.

As he spoke, a terrible sound echoed down the tunnel. It sounded like the roar of rocks grinding against one another. Above came the high-pitched begging of Gwen's brother. 'Please, no! Please!'

Tanner and Gwen ran until they saw the figure of Gor's last soldier standing and peering over a rocky balcony. He was watching something below, and didn't hear their approach until they were almost on him. As he turned, Tanner charged with Gwen, and they both pushed the guard over the ledge. He toppled with a scream, feet first.

Tanner looked over the edge and watched the guard slide down a steep dusty slope fifteen paces high, then scramble to his feet at the bottom. He immediately tried to climb up again, but the slope was sheer and he couldn't get a grip. Geffen was also at the bottom, crouched in a ball and whimpering. Tanner gasped when he realised what they were both so afraid of. The Troiden.

From the dark shadows opposite, a shape

emerged. The Beast was like a huge slug, pulsing with muscle. Its thick, leathery skin was the same grey and black colour as the rock. The creature's face, if you could call it that, consisted of twenty or so stubby tentacles, each ending with a mouth lined with triangular teeth which opened and closed, searching for prey. In the centre of the tentacle-mouths was a bulbous disk the size of Tanner's head, opalescent like the surface of a pearl. *An eye!*

The Troiden butted into the wall of the cavern, and several of its jaws clamped onto the rocks. Tanner heard the grinding noise once more, and saw the teeth sink into the rock, crushing it into showers of dust. Now Tanner understood what had made the marks on the tunnel walls – indeed, what had *made* all the tunnels. This earth-Beast was made for mining.

'Help me!' shouted the soldier, scrambling up. 'Please, don't let it get me!'

The Troiden backed away, then came forward

once more: slow, and deadly, feeling its way. Tanner realised why it wasn't moving straight towards Geffen and the guard.

'It's blind!' he said to Gwen.

She was staring in horror at the sight below. The soldier left his struggle to climb the wall and seized Geffen by the shoulders. He yanked the boy up, and spun him round, then shoved him towards the rock-eating Beast. Geffen sprawled across the ground. He looked up at Gwen.

'Why aren't you helping me?' he called up. 'Why don't you ever help me?'

Gwen let out a cry of anguish and started to scramble down the wall they were leaning against. The Troiden lifted its huge eye, searching blindly for the source of the noise. Tanner gripped her by the wrist and twisted her round roughly.

'No,' he said. 'I won't let you sacrifice yourself. It's too dangerous.'

Below them, Geffen curled into a terrified ball.

The Troiden's tentacle mouths moved towards him.

'I'm coming!' shouted Gwen. She pulled herself free and vaulted over the ledge, sliding down to the bottom, just managing to keep her balance.

'Gwen, no!' Tanner called.

Gwen rushed forward to Geffen's side, and pulled her brother back as one of the mouths reached within a sword's length. 'You have to get to your feet!' she shouted at Geffen.

As the Beast reached for her, she slashed with her rapier, but the sharp blade hardly scratched the tentacles' thick hide. Tanner picked up rocks from the ground and pelted them one after the other at the Beast. But it was hopeless.

The Troiden moved on relentlessly. It was less than thirty paces from the slope now, and the three victims were pressed up against the rock desperately.

'You have to work together!' said Tanner.

'Geffen, stand on your sister's shoulders and reach up to me!'

It took Gwen a moment to understand what he was saying. She looked up the slope, as if weighing the distance, then held her brother's face close to hers and spoke directly at him. He nodded briskly, his head jerking to look at the snorting, shuffling Troiden.

Gwen crouched, facing the slope, and Geffen managed to get both feet on her shoulders. Tanner, lodging his feet against the rockface, leant over the ledge as far as he could and reached down. As Gwen straightened her knees, Geffen stretched up with his hands. Their fingers touched.

But the soldier below was clambering over Gwen, pushing her aside. 'Let me up!' he said.

'Get off!' shouted Gwen.

The soldier didn't listen, and began to pull himself over Geffen's body too, ignoring the boy's shouts of pain. Tanner's fingers broke from Geffen's and the soldier latched onto his wrist, heaving himself up.

Tanner tried to free his arm. As the soldier got a foot on the ledge, he managed to shake himself loose from the man's grasp. He fell away with a jerk, and the soldier plummeted back into the cave. Tanner heard him hit the ground with a thud.

He jumped up, and looked over once more. The soldier had fallen halfway between the slope and the advancing Beast. He lay on his back, moving his head groggily. His eyes opened just as the first of the Troiden's mouths latched onto his shoulder. Then he screamed.

Tanner hardly dared watch as the other mouths shifted to their prey, attaching to different parts of his body. There was a dreadful slurping sound as each mouth took hold and the man's flesh started to pull and pucker, blood bursting and running down his limbs in rivulets. His head fell back on his neck and his eyes rolled as he foamed at the mouth, the pain making his body jerk. More mouths closed around him, and soon there was nothing but the awful sounds of snorting and chewing.

Tanner reached over again, and stretched towards Geffen. Their fingertips brushed. He reached further and grasped the boy's wrist. He leant out with his other hand, and took hold of the other wrist.

'Hold on!' he shouted

With a cry, he pulled with everything he had, gritting his teeth as the fire spread up through his elbow joints and into his shoulder. Gwen was gripping her brother's ankles.

'Pull harder!' she shouted.

Tanner saw the Troiden turn its attention from the soldier's remains and move once more towards his friend.

With his feet pressed against the wall behind, the muscles in his legs felt wrenched apart, and he thought his spine might break. But slowly Geffen was moving upwards.

Sweat was pouring into Tanner's eyes, and he squeezed them shut, feeling the ligaments in his wrist and elbow stretch close to snapping. But he wasn't going to let go.

He saw Gwen had her feet on the slope and had managed to get some purchase, lightening the load on his arms. Geffen reached for the rim with one hand. Tanner let his weight shift backwards, and pulled him the rest of the way. Then Gwen's hand grasped the edge too, and she heaved herself over.

At the bottom, the Troiden growled and snorted, scattering dust from the ceiling.

'You saved me!' sobbed Geffen, throwing his arms around his sister's neck. His voice came out as a muffle. 'You came back for me, after everything I did.'

Gwen hugged her brother tightly. 'Of course I did,' she said.

Suddenly, a series of shrieks sounded through the tunnels, echoing off the walls.

But the noise wasn't human.

'It's Nera!' said Tanner. 'She's bringing down the caves!'

The mountain falls

Chapter Sixteen

He is in danger: Tanner, my Chosen Rider. Even out here, in the mountain air, I know it. His life is almost gone.

The young ones are safe, led down the mountainside by Nera's Rider. The cat-Beast perches by the entrance, uttering her roars that will bring down the mountain for good, that will crush the evil inside. Rocks fall along the tunnel, breaking it apart, closing off Tanner's route to escape.

Gulkien mourns beside me, howling at the sky.

This cannot be our Riders' grave. We must help them. We must.

But what can we do?

The cave echoed with another screech that was piercingly high, then thundered so low that Tanner felt it vibrate through his ribs. He grabbed onto the wall to steady himself as the cavern shuddered.

'We have to get out,' said Gwen.

Rocks began to fall from the ceiling and a long

stalactite broke free above Troiden's pit, smashing down onto the Beast, which writhed in anger and snapped its mouths. The whole mountain shook and groaned.

Geffen pulled away from his sister's embrace. 'I know the way out,' he said. 'I remember from when Vendrake brought me here.'

Vendrake! Where was he? Tanner hadn't seen Derthsin's servant since he'd followed Gor and the other guards.

'You're sure?' said Gwen, interrupting Tanner's thoughts.

Geffen nodded bravely. 'Follow me.'

Gwen's brother led them back through the falling debris. In some places, the walls had already given way, crumbling into piles of rock they had to jump over. With each of Nera's calls, the thunder of falling rocks grew louder.

They passed the junction where Gor had ridden down his own soldier. The body was now half-covered in fallen rocks. Geffen turned into the tunnel where they'd fought the three guards.

Tanner hesitated. 'Are you certain?' he shouted, pointing. 'The general went that way?'

Geffen looked in the direction Tanner was indicating. 'I'm positive,' he said.

'We have to trust him,' Gwen added.

They went after her brother. There was a groan and one of the tunnel walls ahead came down in a wave of rushing rock and dust. Tanner ran, his legs pumping, boots slipping over the uneven ground. He rolled under a falling stone, then dodged left as a piece of the wall came off. Black dust washed over Tanner from behind. The world became solid darkness and his ears were filled with the roar of the mountain collapsing. He sprinted faster, his lungs burning. The tunnels seemed to be heading upwards.

Another piercing shriek from Nera made Tanner fall to his knees. He scrambled up, seeing a long chunk of the ceiling come away in a crash that almost flattened Gwen.

'Nearly there!' called Geffen.

The boy stumbled as a rock clipped his shoulder, knocking him off-balance. Blood streaked down his shoulder.

Tanner passed a familiar archway, and realised where he was: the chamber where Derthsin had spoken with Gor, Vendrake and Captain Brutus. Near the armouries.

'Geffen's right!' shouted Tanner over the roar of the mountain. They reached the armouries and Tanner caught a glimpse of the destruction. Stalactites were crashing onto the forges and fires blazed all about. A black torrent of rocks came down onto the cages, crushing them completely.

Then the whole cavern fell in a whooshing rush, like a gigantic waterfall. The ground and walls were shaking so violently that Tanner couldn't focus on them clearly. They didn't have much time. He had a vague sense of Firepos calling to him, reminding him to be brave.

A square of light came into view ahead, but the

support beams that held up the entranceway were cracking. Its ceiling was already falling in showers of sharp stone that tore at Tanner's face and peppered his back. The others were just shadows ahead. He stumbled through the dust, feeling his way.

A hand snatched at his chest and tugged him aside. 'No!' said Gwen.

Tanner caught his breath and froze. He was standing on the edge of a sheer drop, hundreds of feet up, with the ground shaking beneath his feet. The route by which they'd entered had almost fallen away. Rockfalls cascaded all over the side of the mountain, and clouds of dust rose like mist across the peaks. Far below, he saw Nera stalking the rocks ahead of a convoy of children.

'It wasn't meant to be like this!' said Geffen.

Tanner's foot slipped as the ledge crumbled further, and he gripped the rockface, heart thumping to his throat.

There was no way out.

My heart leaps when I see him running through the cloud of rock and smoke. My Chosen Rider, Tanner — alive! He is coughing, bloody. I see how close the thread of his life came to being cut. Even now, he is straining to breathe, drained from the struggle inside the mountain. I fly to him, and beside me Gulkien howls.

The mountain shook once again, and Geffen grabbed his arm. 'We're going to die!' he cried.

Tanner heard a howl, and two shapes soared through the clouds of dust. His heart lifted. 'It's Gulkien and Firepos!' he shouted.

The Flame Bird cut through the air with powerful strokes of her wings, her beak glinting and her eyes fixed on Tanner. In the darkness of the caves, Tanner could see the tiny flames that flickered on the tips of her feathers. Gulkien howled once more, his fur rippling as his leathery wings cut through the air.

'There's nowhere for them to land,' said Gwen.

A crunch overhead made Tanner press himself

back further against the rock face as boulders the size of cartwheels thundered past, smashing to smithereens hundreds of feet down. They weren't yet safe.

The Beasts moved closer, wings thumping the air, hovering just below Tanner and Gwen. Fist-sized rocks bounced off their bodies, but they held firm.

'We have to jump!' said Tanner.

Firepos shifted in the air, ten feet below. If Tanner misjudged his jump, there wouldn't be any chance of her catching him.

'You go first,' said Geffen, looking down.

Gwen steadied her feet, then launched herself off the ledge, her cloak rippling. She landed horizontally across Gulkien's torso. She gripped his fur and pulled herself upright, swinging her leg over his back. Her Beast gave a low growl of pleasure.

Tanner took a deep breath. He had to do this. He thought of Grandmother Esme, and how proud she'd always been of him. Then he jumped. He thought for a moment he'd overshot, but Firepos jerked sideways and he clenched both fists in her thick feathers. It had never felt so good to be on his Beast and for a moment he hid his face in her feathers.

'Thanks, Firepos,' he murmured. He felt his Beast send warmth out of her body, encasing him. Tanner looked up in time to see Firepos bank away from the cliff face so that Gulkien could manoeuvre closer still. Below, Tanner saw that Castor and the boys were watching.

'Your turn!' shouted Gwen to Geffen. 'Jump!'

To the left of the tunnel entrance a shower of blue-black rocks crashed down as a huge chunk of the mountain disintegrated. Geffen clung to the rock at the end of the tunnel. His whole body was trembling. He looked down at Gulkien, then back into the cavern, as if unsure what to do.

'That way is death!' shouted Tanner. 'You have to be strong, Geffen!'

But Geffen was shaking his head over and over, mumbling something under his breath. 'I can't do it!' he yelled. 'It's too far.'

Gwen tried to take Gulkien nearer, until the tips of his leathery wings were brushing the cliff face. 'Geffen, I can't come closer.'

Suddenly, the mountain groaned, and Geffen stumbled. He fell backwards, and scrambled to his knees, staring with wide eyes at his sister on Gulkien's back. He reached out a trembling hand.

'Help me!' He was crying openly now, not caring who saw.

The air seemed to shift, and a roar sounded from above like a thousand waves crashing on a beach. Gwen tried to steer Gulkien closer to her brother, but he wheeled away, sending out a breeze that flattened Geffen's hair against his scalp.

'No, Gulkien! Come on!' Gwen cried desperately. Gulkien sent out a warning snarl that let her know he had no intention of flying them both closer to their deaths. There was an almighty groan and a huge section of the peak collapsed in on itself, and a slab of rock, fifty paces across, slid off.

Geffen was still on his knees when the shower of rock descended. He was flattened to the ground, dust piling around him, rocks the size of his skull pounding the boy's body. Firepos cried with distress as they watched Gwen's brother roll onto his back, his head tipping over the edge of the ledge. His eyes rolled back in his head, his hair matted white with dust. Blood ran from the corner of his mouth, dripping into the depths below. Then a final rock fall buried him.

Gwen sat wrapped in a blanket, staring into the flames of the kitchen fire. They were back in Castor's village, in the house he'd once shared with his family. Tanner brought a bowl of broth to her, and she took it without looking up. Tear tracks stained her cheeks.

Tanner looked out of the window to where Firepos, Gulkien and Nera lay together in the ruins of Castor's garden. The Flame Bird blinked slowly, the moonlight reflecting off her feathers. She caught his eye and sent out a call to him. *Take heart. This too will pass.* Tanner shook himself; he didn't know if he could believe what his Beast was telling him. Gulkien's ears twitched, as if he was struggling to hear Gwen's thoughts. Tanner settled himself beside Castor, who was sharpening his dagger with a whetting stone.

They'd looked for Geffen's body until nightfall, but long before they found anything the horizon had become streaked with orange and fireball red, and the Northern Mountains had turned yellow and pink below them, and Tanner had known it was pointless. The light cast long shadows on the uneven rock.

'Come on,' he'd said to the others, eventually. 'We need to go. Geffen's buried and there's nothing we can do about it.' He'd placed a hand on Gwen's shoulder and she'd climbed stiffly to her feet, her hands bloodied from searching among the rocks. She'd nodded once; her admission that the search was without hope.

They'd returned to Colton with the boys they'd rescued. The mood had been sombre and quiet as they'd flown there on the back of Firepos and Gulkien, or ridden on Nera's back.

'Geffen's gone.' said Gwen, breaking into Tanner's thoughts. 'He saved my life and I couldn't do anything for him.'

'He'd understand,' said Tanner. *Now we've all lost someone close to us*, he thought.

Outside, Nera stood up and stretched, her great muscles heaving and rippling under her golden fur. Castor put his dagger in his belt and strode out of the house into the darkness.

'Is he all right?' Gwen asked.

'I'm not sure.' Tanner thought back to the flash of pain he thought he'd seen in Castor before they went into the armoury. There was still a secret hiding there. 'Let's leave him be.'

Tanner went over and sat beside his friend. 'Geffen saved all our lives, you know,' he said. 'After everything he did wrong, he guided us out of the tunnels to safety. You should remember that.'

Tanner put his arm around Gwen and stared into the flames. Despair clawed at his heart. Now Derthsin had two pieces of the mask, his powers would be greater than ever. Tanner had already seen that through Vendrake, he had some kind of hold over Firepos. Vendrake had disappeared – was he still alive? *If we come up against him again, what will be the cost?* And General Gor was out there, working for his dark master. At least he and his friends had the map. But Tanner was beginning to wonder what difference that made. If Gor knew roughly where the pieces were, then they would have to face him again and he might find the other two pieces long before Tanner and his friends could travel the kingdom. And once all the pieces were reunited, Anoret could be summoned – the first ever Beast of Avantia. And the most powerful.

That's how the legends had it. If he came back, could Anoret be made into Derthsin's creature? Tanner wasn't prepared to find out – he had to get the pieces of the mask back, whatever it took.

'He's probably already on his way to the next piece,' he muttered.

'What? What are you talking about?' Gwen said, pulling away. Her face froze over. 'You're not still thinking about the Mask of Death, are you? That's exactly what it is – a bringer of death! Look at everything that's happened!' She stood up and walked out of the cottage, following Castor. Tanner watched her leave.

Through the window, he saw Castor stroking Nera's flank, his head rested in her fur. Gwen went to stand beside him, and Tanner watched them talking quietly. When Tanner had first met Castor, the arrogant bully in the village square, he never would have dreamt they might one day fight together, but then fate had taken all sorts of strange turns since the day his father had died. Would Gwen still be willing to fight by their side, too?

Tanner closed his eyes, but he could still see flames burning through his eyelids and a face hovering in the fire. The face of Derthsin. It was as though the destruction and devastation haunted him still.

One day, he promised himself. *The fires will stop.* Despite the exhaustion that seeped into his body, he knew he had to carry on. He imagined he could hear Derthsin laughing at him – mocking him. Tanner's hands balled into fists.

'This isn't the end of it, Derthsin,' he said. 'Not by a long way.' As he spoke, a blinding pain filled his head and he squeezed his eyes tightly shut. He could hear Firepos cawing with concern. A vision plunged behind his eyelids – a twisting scar, snaking down a man's throat. Derthsin's servant.

Vendrake's smirk widened into a grin.

'We're waiting for you,' the man said. Beyond his shoulder, Tanner glimpsed the vulture that pulled his chariot.

Tanner snapped his eyes open. Gwen and Castor had come back inside. He hadn't even heard them. Gwen stared at him, concern creasing her brow. Even Castor looked worried.

'What is it?' Castor demanded. 'Tell us.'

Vendrake had been carrying a piece of the mask, stroking it. The mask had been surrounded by a halo of light that seemed to call to Tanner. He felt sick to his stomach. He'd wanted to reach out to the piece of the mask, to put it on. Could he tell his friends how he'd wanted to be the wearer of the mask?

'I was thinking about Vendrake, that's all,' he said quickly.

Beyond the window of the cottage, Firepos took to the night skies, flames licking around the edges of her feathers. She called out strongly to

Tanner. *Our fates await us*. He knew Firepos was right. But what did fate have in store for him?

Gwen and Castor watched Tanner silently.

'I don't know what else is out there,' he said. 'I can't promise we'll make it through this alive.'

Castor shrugged, with all the casual bravado of a boy who had spent his life waiting to fight with his sword.

'I don't care,' he said. 'I'm in this now, and I'm not coming back to my village again until I come back a hero. Even if you have to carry my body here. I want to grind Derthsin beneath my heel.' He twisted his foot against the ground, churning up dust.

Gwen stepped closer to Tanner. 'I want to carry on fighting, too,' she said quietly. 'I've lost so much already. I don't want to lose this battle.' She gazed past Tanner, over the landscape beyond the cottage window. 'I love my kingdom.' Her glance snapped back to Tanner. 'And I know you do, too. Let's find the pieces of the mask.'

Tanner felt his hands clench into fists.

'Whatever it takes?' he asked.

Castor nodded and Gwen pushed her cloak aside, to reveal the throwing axes in her belt.

'Whatever it takes,' she agreed.

Derthsin was out there, somewhere, waiting for them.

We're coming for you, Tanner thought.

The Chronicles of Avantia

Tanner's story continues in *Call to War*.

Avantia burns in the fires of war. Derthsin's evil armies swarm the land, and Tanner, Gwen and Castor, and their powerful Beasts, are all that stand in their way.

Will they encounter more Beasts on their treacherous journey to the Southern Caves to find the next piece of the Mask of Death? And will the dark forces that seek control of Tanner prevent the Riders from fulfilling their destiny…?

Read on for an exciting preview of *Call to War*, the next adventure in the Chronicles of Avantia…

Chapter One

The golden chain turned slowly as Gwen held it in front of her face. Scratched and worn at the edges, the locket still glittered in the dawn light. Gwen's blue eyes were bright and focused, her white-blonde hair tucked behind her ears, still disheveled from where she had slept on the ground with her wolf-Beast, Gulkien. Behind Tanner, Castor was just waking up.

Their three Beasts – Gulkien, Nera and Firepos – stood guard at the edge of the forest clearing. Firepos was a huge Flame Bird, her feathers shimmering gold as tiny flames flared at her wingtips.

Beside her, Gulkien stretched his leathery wings as his lips curled back and he ran his tongue over long fangs.

Tanner could sense the message Firepos sent to him across the air: *A new day brings fresh challenges.* Tanner and his Beast had been together ever since he'd been a young boy. Together, they'd lived through the death of his father at the hands of the evil warrior, Derthsin, and the kidnap of his mother. Firepos had helped Tanner survive.

A crow cawed. Tanner recognised that sound: the screech of a carrion bird, searching for a corpse. He waited as Gwen traced her finger around the edge of the locket, tapping a hidden button. Something clicked, and the front cover opened.

Castor came over to see, his golden hair clumped with leaves and dirt where it curled around his temples. 'Why are we up so early?' he grumbled, wiping sleep from his eyes.

Gwen carefully placed the open locket on a clear patch on the ground. She plucked out a tiny gossamer square that shimmered and sparkled like river water in the dim light. 'We have to keep moving,' she said, without looking up. 'Open the map.'

Tanner reached into his tunic and slowly

unfurled the parchment map they had used in the previous few days. His hands steady and being careful with the cracked edges, he laid the map between them. Gwen shook open the gossamer, which opened like a tiny sail, and placed it over the parchment. Behind them, Tanner heard Firepos rustle her wings. Gulkien sniffed and paced, while Nera's wide cat-eyes scanned the forest canopy.

Castor sighed. 'I don't see anything.'

'Be patient,' Gwen said.

Tanner leant close with Gwen. The gossamer shimmered like a wax skin, blurring the colours of mountains and forests, smearing the lines of roads and the names of towns and villages.

'It makes things harder to see,' Castor said, craning over the top of their heads, 'not easier.'

'You know how this works,' Tanner said, still watching the map. 'It should show us where to find the third piece of the mask.'

'Right,' Castor said. 'So we can lose it like we lost the other two pieces.'

Tanner tried to ignore him.

'Castor, please,' Gwen said. 'Just wait...'

The wind blew harder, and when the branches overhead parted, a shaft of daylight lit the map. A tiny picture blotted onto the gossamer, like an ink ghost, as if the daylight had brightened the world just enough that they could see something that had been there all along. A small image glowed like a gemstone.

When Tanner peered closer, he saw the outline of a leathery cheek and the edge of a brow – a piece of a small, empty face. Tanner shivered, but there it was, hiding near the Southern Caves: the third piece of the Mask of Death.

Tanner had been tracking the pieces of the mask ever since his grandmother, Esme, had died at the hands of Derthsin's general, Gor. She'd told him to go to Jonas the mapmaker. He hadn't found Jonas, but he had found Gwen and her brother – adopted twins of the mapmaker. Then he and Gwen had been led to Castor by their Beasts. It was as if the three of them were meant to be together, fighting Derthsin – the man who had survived burning in a volcano. The man who wanted control of the Beasts and, through them, to cast fear over Avantia. To make the kingdom his own.

They'd fought hard to snatch the pieces of the mask from Derthsin, but Castor was right – they'd failed. They didn't have a single piece – General Gor wore the pieces hung from his belt. Mocking them.

The mask was said to be made from the face of the first Beast of Avantia, Anoret. *We have to get them back*, Tanner swore to himself. *For the sake of all that is good in this kingdom*. It may have been made up of feudal towns and villages, scraping together an existence, but it was the place Esme had loved with all her heart. For the sake of his murdered grandmother, Tanner wouldn't allow Avantia to crumble.

Gwen tapped a north-south line on the map.

'This path links the armoury, where we saw Derthsin's poor slaves making weapons and armour, with the Southern Caves.'

'They may have built the armoury there,' Tanner said, thinking aloud, 'so they could equip an army to conquer the south.'

Castor said, 'I don't like this.'

As Tanner rolled up the parchment map, he looked over the flat greens of Avantia's grassland and the darker blotches of forest that cut across in clumps at the centre and edges of the map. He saw drawings of hills in browns and greys that led to sharp mountains, and as Tanner closed the map, he wondered if every blue-line river flowed to a lake or out to the open sea beyond the map's borders. There were still so many parts of this kingdom that Tanner had never even visited, yet he knew he would be willing to fight for all of Avantia. Anything rather than give it to Derthsin.

Tanner returned the map to Gwen and

touched her shoulder. Her eyes were swollen, as if she had barely slept.

'I'm fine,' she said. She put her gossamer away and hooked the locket back round her neck.

'Come on,' Tanner said. 'It's time to go.'

'Wait,' Castor said. 'I'm part of this team, too, and I think we should wait. I have better instincts. I'm telling you, we need to wait until the sun burns off the morning dew.'

'You have better instincts?' Tanner said. 'We don't have time to wait around, Castor. General Gor has two pieces of the mask.'

'And we all know whose fault that is,' muttered Castor.

Anger flared in Tanner's chest. He recalled General Gor taunting him at the mines. *You have nothing to look forward to but your deaths*, he'd told them. He'd almost been right – there had been too many soldiers and Tanner had been helpless to retake the mask pieces from him. But in the mines, Castor had been brave and selfless. He'd helped Tanner save the boys, even though Gwen's brother had been lost. *We need that Castor, not this arrogant, disgruntled one*, thought Tanner.

Gwen put a hand on Castor's shoulder. 'Please Castor, don't fight about this now.'

Tanner went to Firepos and held her bright feathers to climb onto her back.

'We don't have a choice,' Tanner said. 'We have to start again. It's time to go.'

The Chronicles of Avantia
book 1

First Hero
Out Now!

The Chronicles of Avantia
book 3

Call to War
Out Now!